Foto: Malte Bastian

Emer O'Sullivan, *1957, aufgewachsen in Dublin, hat dort und in Berlin
Germanistik und Anglistik studiert. Sie war Stipendiatin für Kinder- und
Jugendliteratur der Berliner Stiftung Preußische Seehandlung und arbeitet
jetzt am Institut für Jugendbuchforschung der Johann-Wolfgang-von-
Goethe-Universität in Frankfurt a. M.
Dietmar Rösler, *1951, aufgewachsen in Emden, Studium in Berlin.
Zwischen 1977 und 1996 Arbeit an den Fachbereichen Germanistik des
University College Dublin, der Freien Universität Berlin und des
King's College London. Seither Professor für Deutsch als Fremdsprache
an der Universität Gießen.
Von den Autoren liegen außerdem vor: «I like you – und du?», «It could
be worse – oder?», «Mensch, be careful!», «Butler & Graf» und
«Butler, Graf & Friends: Umwege» (Bände 20323 / 20374 / 20417 / 20480 /
20647).
Von Dietmar Rösler bei rotfuchs: «Störtebeker im Netz. Eine Science-
Fiction?» (Band 20803).

Emer O'Sullivan / Dietmar Rösler

Butler, Graf & Friends: Nur ein Spiel?

****

Ein deutsch-englischer
Krimi

Rowohlt

31.–33. Tausend September 1999

Originalausgabe
Veröffentlicht im Rowohlt Taschenbuch Verlag GmbH,
Reinbek bei Hamburg, Juni 1990
Copyright © 1990 by Rowohlt Taschenbuch Verlag GmbH,
Reinbek bei Hamburg
Umschlagfoto Sebastian Kusenberg
Alle Rechte vorbehalten
Gesetzt aus der Garamond (Linotronic 500)
Gesamtherstellung Clausen & Bosse, Leck
Printed in Germany
ISBN 3 499 20531 9

Die Schreibweise entspricht den Regeln
der neuen Rechtschreibung.

Inhaltsverzeichnis

Chapter one

****

in which Sakina feels something is wrong
und in dem Florian sich im Fernsehen bewundert

Eröffnungsfanfare. Titel: SUPERCHAIN – The Super European Quiz Show. Dann die Stimme aus dem Off: «Ladies and gentlemen, welcome your hostess Ginger Marley.» Gleich kommen wir, gleich kommen wir. Florian saß aufgeregt in einem Sessel im Wohnzimmer der Familie Butler, während Maddy und Sakina scheinbar ganz locker auf dem Boden ausgestreckt lagen, aber auch sie starrten gebannt auf den Bildschirm. Sakina was stuffing her face with crisps. Still staring at the screen, she handed the bag to Florian.

Auf dem Bildschirm hatte Ginger Marley kurz die Spielregeln erklärt. Jetzt stellte sie gerade die Kandidaten vor.

«Here is the team that calls itself ‹The Jugglers› – from London we have Sakina, Una here is from Dublin, and from Germany, from Berlin – Florian.»

Tosender Beifall. Dabei waren kaum Zuschauer im Studio gewesen, als die Sendung aufgenommen worden war.

«Just imagine», Maddy commented, «thousands of people all over Europe are looking at you on TV at this very moment. Amazing what satellites can do, isn't it?»

Toll seh ich aus, der blaue Pullover wirkt echt gut, dachte Florian, während er eine Hand voll Kartoffelchips aus der Tüte nahm. Er achtete kaum auf die Vorstellung der gegnerischen Mannschaft. Seine *Vorbereitung* in Berlin hatte sich ausgezahlt.

Vor fünf Wochen – in der Woche, bevor diese erste Sendung von SUPERCHAIN in London aufgenommen worden war – war er jeden Tag in einem Riesen-Elektroladen in Berlin gewesen. Immer mit anderen Klamotten. Dort war er vor den Kameras, die den Laden überwachen, auf und ab gegangen und hatte auf dem Bildschirm überprüft, welche seiner Sachen besonders fernsehtauglich waren. Natürlich ganz unauffällig, wie er meinte. Bis am sechsten Tag einer der Verkäufer ihn mit ‹Hallo, Fernsehstar› begrüßte.

«That's not him, that's the wrong fellow», Sakina interrupted Florian's self-admiration. «I don't believe it», she raised her voice, «look at him, Florian. The fellow in the green jacket. He's not the one who was there when the show was recorded!»

«Das geht doch gar nicht» und «That's not possible», riefen Florian and Maddy gleichzeitig. «Are you sure?», Maddy asked, «after all, they've only shown him for a few seconds so far.»

«Of course I'm sure.» Sakina replied quickly, «I was there, wasn't I?»

«Well, so was Florian. What does he have to say about it?», Maddy wanted to know.

«Keine Ahnung. Ich hab ihn mir nicht ordentlich angesehen. Konzentriert euch lieber auf unsere tolle Show da», war das Einzige, was Florian zu sagen hat.

Maddy and Sakina raised their eyes to heaven. Honestly, these vain fellows! Sakina remembered that they were recording the programme on video anyway, so they could look at that shot again later. Maybe her eyes were playing tricks on her.

Auf dem Bildschirm hatte die Spielleiterin inzwischen die Vorstellung der beiden Mannschaften beendet. Gerade erzählte sie von dem Traumpreis, der den Sieger erwartete:

«The winning team will fly to New York on Concord, spending two days in the Big Apple before travelling on to Florida. There they will stay in Orlando, visit the world's largest tourist attraction, Disney World, experience the natural wonders of the Everglades National Park and the Florida Keys and visit the Kennedy Space Centre at Cape Canaveral, to name but a few of the highlights.»

Dann begann die erste Runde.

Sakina grabbed the crisps back from Florian and started eating them again. She was on television!

«And now, the first question in the first episode of our European Quiz goes to the Argonauts, to Carla from Denmark», said Ginger Marley. «Carla, for one point: If you fly from Munich to Vienna, are you flying north, south, east or west?»

«East», antwortete Carla, ohne zu zögern.

«South», said Maddy at the same time in front of the television. Her team was in the quarterfinal in two days' time, and she used every possible opportunity to rehearse for it.

«Correct, one point», said Ginger Marley. «Shit», said Maddy.

«She probably knew that because she's been there», Sakina consoled her friend. «The Scottish fellow on the Argonauts' team is coming up next. He's really good, he scores a treble twenty in darts. And after that…»

«Sakina, halt die Klappe», unterbrach Florian sie, «ich will das sehen und nicht deine Zusammenfassung hören.»

Sakina sulked and didn't say a word for a couple of minutes while the Scottish fellow completed his task. Her mind went back to what she had seen earlier. She could have sworn that the fellow who was shown on the screen in the introduction was not the same one who was there when the show was being recorded.

«Mann, hat der ein Glück gehabt», kommentierte Florian den erfolgreichen Darts-Wurf. «Na», wandte er sich an Sakina, «jetzt werden wir ja sehen, ob dein Typ vertauscht worden ist.» Er lachte.

Ginger Marley kündigte auf dem Bildschirm die dritte Aufgabe für die Argonauts an: «Your team has got the first two tasks right so far, Andy, and you know that three correct ones in a row means that your team will get a link of the chain. The first link of the first chain. Who knows, maybe it will be your first link on the way to Florida.»

Die Kamera konzentrierte sich ganz auf Ginger Marley. Moment mal, dachte Florian, als sie direkt nach der Aufnahme Ausschnitte aus der Sendung gesehen hatten, war doch dauernd auf die Gesichter der Kandidaten umgeschnitten worden – oder irrte er sich?

«Are you ready?», Ginger Marley asked. «We are going to show you two short film clips, one after the other. They are identical except for three small shanges. You have to spot at least two of them for your team to get that link.»

Die kurzen Szenen liefen ab.

«The man was wearing a green jumper in the first clip but it was blue in the second one, and there were no flowers on the table in the second clip», kam die Antwort, während der zweite Film noch lief.

«Well done! Very well done, indeed. That's the third correct answer in a row from the Argonauts. The first link of their chain goes to them», jubilierte Ginger Marley, während die Kamera sie in Großaufnahme zeigte. Dann sah man die Kette der Argonauts, bei der jetzt das erste Glied erleuchtet war.

«Why do they show her and not Andy?», asked Maddy. «He was the one who answered the question.»

«That's because it isn't the Andy we know», insisted Sakina and opened another bag of crisps. «We've seen all the others in close-up when they were answering their questions, but not him.»

«You sound like you think they are trying to hide him», replied Maddy and laughed, «that's ridiculous. You didn't see him during his round because he answered his film clip question so quickly that the second clip was still running», she explained.

«We'll see.» Sakina wasn't convinced.

Auch für den Rest dieser Runde war der zweifelhafte Andy kaum genau oder lange genug zu sehen. Die drei stritten sich fast, ob das nun Zufall war oder nicht, während die Jugglers – Florians und Sakinas Mannschaft – in der ersten Runde insgesamt drei Glieder der Kette eroberten, ebenso viele wie die gegnerische Mannschaft, die Argonauts.

Sakina felt that something was wrong. She couldn't concentrate fully on the other three rounds of the game, although she had performed particularly well in one of them. Maddy kept saying to her: «You look great on the box. A real natural.» She was almost sure that the Andy on the screen wasn't the Andy they had seen in the studio during the recording. But how could she explain it? What was the difference between them?

«Well, what a terrific performance by both teams. And what a close finish», fasste Ginger Marley auf dem Bildschirm das Spiel zusammen. «14 links of the chain for the Jugglers who were just beaten by the Argonauts with 15 links. Our congratulations to the Argonauts for a tremendous performance and our commiserations to the Jugglers, who put a splendid fight but who came up against a very strong team indeed. We shall see the Argonauts again in the quarterfinals. And if we look at the number of links the Jugglers managed to get, it might just be enough to qualify them for the Consolation Match – the last chance for the two losing teams with the highest scores to play against one another for a place in the quarterfinal. A big ‹thank you› to our viewers all over Europe for watching ‹SUPER-CHAIN – The Super European Quiz Show›. We hope you enjoyed it as much as we did. See you again same time, same place, next week. Cheerio!» The titles rolled.

Florian lehnte sich zurück. Sie hatten verloren, obwohl sie fast alles richtig gemacht hatten. Mist, dass sie gleich auf einen so starken Gegner gestoßen waren. Seine Gedanken wanderten zum nächsten Tag, wo sie in der Trostrunde um den letzten freien Platz im Viertelfinale kämpfen würden. Das war schon komisch, das Fernsehen zeigte gerade das erste Ausscheidungsspiel und nächste Woche um dieselbe Zeit das zweite. Dabei waren schon sieben Spiele fertig und morgen sollte im Studio die Trostrunde aufgezeichnet werden.

Maddy pressed the ‹stop› button on the remote control of the video recorder and then started to rewind the tape.

«Congratulations you two», she said to her two friends. «How did you like seeing yourselves on telly?»

«Wenn ich in der zweiten Runde bloß schneller geraten hätte, dann hätten wir ein Glied mehr gehabt…», sagte Florian, «aber sonst fand ich, dass ich stark rübergekommen bin.»

«Herr Graf – always the modest gentleman», Maddy commented sarcastically and added: «I'm glad you thought Sakina looked good on the screen, too.»

Florian wurde rot. «Sakina sah natürlich im Fernsehen genauso schön aus wie im richtigen Leben», antwortete er, «mal sehen, was für eine Erscheinung Miss Supercool uns nächste Woche hier bieten wird.»

«Ms. Supercool, if you don't mind», Maddy snapped back.

«Can't you two shut up for a moment», Sakina interrupted, throwing the empty crisp bag at them. The video had stopped rewinding and she asked Maddy to press the ‹play› button. «I want to have a closer look at this Andy fellow.»

They played the opening sequence again. «See», Sakina said, «I told you it wasn't him. The real Andy was more handsome than he is. He had lovely eyes.»

«Sakina, if you gave that as one of the differences in the question with the two film clips I don't think it would be accepted. Maybe that kind of question has gone to your head and you are just imagining that they've changed something. Is everything else the same?», Maddy asked sceptically.

«You don't believe me, do you?», demanded Sakina. «Well Florian, you were there, what do you think now?»

«Ich weiß nicht, das ging eben alles so schnell», sagte Florian, «spiel es doch noch mal, aber in Zeitlupe.»

Maddy rewound the tape again, and pressed the ‹slow play› button. Florian starrte auf den Bildschirm. Tack – tack. Ganz langsam wechselten die Bilder auf dem Schirm. «Freeze!», Sakina ordered when Andy was in full sight. Maddy pressed the ‹pause› button.

«Vielleicht hat Sakina doch Recht», sagte Florian nach einer Weile, «vielleicht ist das nicht der Typ, der im Studio war.» Er überlegte einen Moment. «Aber falls sie Recht haben sollte – wie ist das möglich?», fragte er.

«And why would anyone want to swop a candidate in a quiz show?», Maddy wondered.

Zweites Kapitel

****

in dem Florian so tut als ob
and in which nobody tells Sakina anything

«Just don't start imagining you have discovered something suspicious», were Maddy's parting words to Sakina as she left the Butler's house.

«What does she think she's discovered?» Maddy's mother had turned up from nowhere. «You three aren't going to get involved in some funny business again, are you?» The memory of the swopped floppy discs still made Mrs Butler feel weak at the knees.

«Only a case of mistaken identity», mischte sich Florian ein. «I mean… Maddy didn't recognize me on the television. She says I'm much more handsome in real live.» Er grinste sie an. «Anyway, I have to go to bed now, I have a hard day in the studio tomorrow.» Er ging die Treppe hinauf.

«That's what you get when you aren't good enough to win your Qualifying Round like we did», Maddy called after him and smiled maliciously, «you have to work overtime in the Consolation Match. Well, off you go then to get your beauty sleep.» She turned to her mother. «You should have seen him when the quiz was on, Mum. He's so vain it's just unbelievable. He sat there admiring himself the whole time.»

«I'm sure you are exaggerating», Mrs Butler thought her daughter should be nicer to the German lad, «but I'm looking forward to seeing it myself. You did record it, didn't you?»

«Yes Mum», said Maddy.

Florian konnte nicht gleich einschlafen. Seine Gedanken gingen zwei Monate zurück, zu dem Tag, als Maddy ihm die Anzeige ‹YOUNG EUROPEAN TEAMS WANTED FOR A TELEVISION QUIZ SHOW IN LONDON› geschickt hatte. Er hatte gedacht, sie wollte ihn veräppeln. Allgemeinbildung war nun wirklich nicht seine Stärke. Er hatte Manni die Anzeige gezeigt, und der in seiner praktischen Art meinte nur, umsonst nach London und Maddy und Sakina besuchen und dazu noch im Fernsehen auftreten – das sei doch Spitze. Sie wollten auch noch Silvia aus seiner Klasse für die Idee begeistern, die die Schülerzeitung machte und außerdem ein wandelndes Lexikon war. Aber sie hatte gerade einen Praktikumsplatz bei einer Berliner Zeitung gefunden. Maddy hatte dann mehr Informationen besorgt und herausgefunden, dass das wirklich ein ungewöhnliches Quiz war. Es ging nicht nur um Wissensfragen, sondern auch um Geschicklichkeit und Beobachtungsgabe.

A couple of streets away Sakina was lying awake in bed. Don't be ridiculous, she was saying to herself, it's so unlikely that there was a swop. And if it wasn't the original fellow, if they had had to substitute someone else for the real Andy and retake the scenes with the substitute, they must have a pretty good reason. They will probably tell us all about it in the studio tomorrow. She tried to go to sleep.

Nach einiger Zeit hatte sich Florian mit der Quiz-Idee angefreundet. Gesucht wurden Gruppen mit drei Teilnehmern aus drei verschiedenen Ländern. Wobei das englische Fernsehen England, Wales, Schottland und Nordirland als eigene Länder zählte. Wie beim Fußball. Allerdings durften nicht alle drei

Mitglieder eines Teams Englisch als Muttersprache haben. So kamen Maddy, Sakina, Manni und Florian auf die Idee, Maddys Freunde Una aus der Republik Irland und Henk aus Holland einzuladen und zwei Gruppen zu bilden, die ‹Jugglers› – das waren Florian, Una und Sakina – und die ‹Floppies› – das waren Maddy, Manni und Henk, alle drei Computer-Freaks.

Maddy was sitting in the living room. The house was quiet, everyone was probably asleep. She stared at the map of Europe. Over and over again she repeated the names of the capital cities and main rivers, trying to memorize them. Neither she nor Manni had a clue about geography, and even Henk, who seemed to know everything else, admitted that it was his weak spot, too. The Floppies had made it to the quarterfinal easily – the opposition hadn't been very good – but now in the quarterfinal… She tried to concentrate. Bucharest is the capital of Romania, Warsaw is the capital of Poland – would she ever get it right? She stayed up late into the night.

Es klopfte ziemlich laut. Florian zog sich die Decke über den Kopf.

«Florian», it was Mrs Butler, «Florian, wake up, it's time for breakfast. That nice girl will be here to pick you up in half an hour.»

That nice girl war Joanne, eine Studentin, die beim Fernsehen als *contestant coordinator* arbeitete; sie war dafür zuständig, dass alle Kandidaten zur richtigen Zeit an der richtigen Stelle waren. Florian mochte sie. Er wurde gleich ein bisschen wacher. Er zog sich an, ging in die Küche, aber er wollte nichts essen, denn er war plötzlich sehr nervös.

«Got the collywobbles, then?», lachte Mrs Butler, «I'm sure you'll be just fine.»

Florian hatte zwar keine Ahnung, was *colly* oder irgendwelche anderen *wobbles* waren, aber wenn *collywobbles* Mrs Butler davon abhielten, ihn zum Frühstück mit den fetten Würstchen voll zu stopfen, dann konnten sie nur was Gutes sein.

«Do you know what the capital of Romania is?» Maddy had just come down the stairs, yawning. Even though she had been up very late, she couldn't sleep on.

«Dracula-City», antwortete Florian.

Maddy tried to give him a dirty look but it wasn't easy with eyes that would only open halfway. «Try again», she said.

«Budapest», sagte der.

«You'll never make it to the quarterfinal», she commented while she poured some muesli into a bowl.

Pünktlich um halb acht klingelte es. «Good morning, Mrs Butler», sagte Joanne und: «Na, Florian, gut in Form?» Sie studierte Deutsch, für sie war das Quiz nur ein Sommerjob, und sie nutzte jede Gelegenheit, mit den deutschen Teilnehmern Deutsch zu reden.

«Na ja, okay, nur ein paar *collywobbles*», sagte Florian.

«*Collywobbles*, eh? Was du so alles auf Englisch kannst», staunte Joanne, während sie zum Auto gingen.

«It's Bucharest!», Maddy shouted after them.

Im Auto erzählte Joanne Florian, dass er gestern auf dem Bildschirm ganz ausgezeichnet ausgesehen habe. Florian fand das auch. Sie holten Sakina ab, die schon auf dem Bürgersteig auf sie wartete.

«Hey, Joanne», she said even before anyone could say ‹hello›, «who was that fellow we saw on the telly last night? He wasn't the Andy we know, was he? I mean, he wasn't the one who was in the studio when they recorded us playing against the Argonauts.»

«Hello, Sakina», sagte Joanne. Florian beobachtete sie genau. War sie nicht ein wenig rot geworden? Schien sie mit ihrer Antwort einen Moment zu lange zu zögern?

«What gave you that idea?», she said. «Of course it was the Andy you know, who else could it have been? You were there when the show was recorded. You saw it with your own eyes.»

«But we…» Sakina wanted to go on but Florian interrupted her.

«Come on Sakina, get into the car, we still have to pick up Una.» Komm Mädchen, mach kein Theater, dachte er. Joanne weiß nichts oder will nichts wissen. Er warf Sakina einen beschwörenden Blick zu.

«Yes, we'd better hurry if we want to pick up Una in time», sagte Joanne. Sakina stieg ein.

Una had arrived from Dublin late the night before and was staying with one of her aunts in North London. She was pleased to see the three of them again, especially the nice German bloke. Maddy had told her a lot about him beforehand, and not all of it had been positive, but when she met him for the first time she was impressed.

«Hi, everyone», she said when she got into the car. «How did you like the show yesterday?» Her aunt had recorded it for her and she had looked at it late the night before.

Florian mochte ihren Dubliner Akzent fast so gern wie den schottischen von Maddys Cousine aus Edinburgh. Sie redeten eine Weile darüber, wie toll es war, sich selbst im Fernsehen zu sehen, und dann sagte Una eher beiläufig: «By the way, I don't know if I was imagining things or not, but that fellow Andy looked a bit odd, didn't he? Not like the Andy I remember from the studio. Was it the same bloke?»

Florian und Sakina hielten den Atem an. Joanne zögerte einen Moment und sagte freundlich:

«Funny you should say that, Una. Of course it was the same bloke – who else could it have been? But Sakina here asked that question, too. Sometimes the make-up and the lights make people look a bit different on the screen.» Sie wandte sich Florian zu: «Was meinst du denn? Kam er dir auch komisch vor?»

«Hey, stop talking Kraut language», Una protested, «I like the Germans», she smiled at Florian, «but I can't speak a word of their awful language.»

«No», sagte Florian zu Joanne, «I didn't notice anything odd. He looked okay, to me.»

Sakina's mouth fell open and she just stared at him.

«Maybe it's *kulturspezifisch* – sorry Una! I don't know what it is in English. I have a teacher who says everything has something to do with the culture you come from. He goes on and on about it. So maybe Irish and Asian females have a certain way of looking at young English gentlemen.»

«*You* can't complain about lack of attention from Irish and Asian females», Joanne said quickly.

Florian sagte keinen Pieps und drehte sich auch nicht um. So sah er nicht, dass die beiden auf den Rücksitzen mit roten Köpfen dasaßen.

Joanne brachte die drei zum *make-up room*. «I have to go to a production meeting», she told them as she left.

Sakina assumed that the make-up girl wouldn't understand German and tried to string a German sentence together: «Was soll das? Why on earth… Warum hast du das gesagt, dass du glaubst, dass es der richtige Andy ist?», she asked Florian, annoyed that she couldn't express herself better in his language.

«Na ja, entweder glaubt sie, was sie sagt, oder sie lügt. Und wenn sie mehr weiß, als sie sagt, dann ist es vielleicht nicht schlecht, wenn ich so tue, als sei ich auf ihrer Seite.»

«For God's sake, stop krauting», Una was annoyed. «Florian's English is good enough.»

Florian beugte sich zu ihr hinüber und flüsterte: «Secret language. It's important. I'll tell you later.» Una liked that.

«Was machst du da?», Sakina said deliberately in German. She knew Una didn't like her speaking it to Florian.

«Ich muss ihr doch sagen, was ich dir gesagt habe.» Sakina sah ihn skeptisch an. Jetzt sah auch Una ihn skeptisch an. Florian saß verlegen zwischen ihnen.

«Next», said the make-up girl. Florian sprang auf.

«You'll ruin your eyes, love», Mrs Butler said to her daughter.

«You usually say that when I'm sitting at the computer», Maddy responded without looking up from *Knowledge from A to Z*, the book she had been reading for the past two hours. «Do you know who invented the phone?», she asked.

«Someone who didn't have a daughter with friends in Germany», her mother said. Their last phone bill had been pretty high while Maddy was organizing them to come over to London for the quiz, and there had been scenes about it. Maddy didn't say anything.

«Why don't you put down the book and go out?», her mother asked. «A bit of fresh air would do you the world of good. You shouldn't be doing so much work preparing yourself for the quiz. After all, it is only a game.»

The phone rang. Mrs Butler answered it. «It's one of your phone-loving, quizzing Germans», she said.

It was Manni.

«Hallo Maddy, ich wollte bloß sagen, ich komme morgen

Abend an. Die haben mich in einem Hotel gleich neben dem Studio untergebracht. Henk wohnt da auch, hat mir Derek, der *contestant coordinator*, erzählt, und er kommt auch morgen Abend. Florian wohnt nicht da, nicht?»

«No, he arrived the day before yesterday and he's staying with us. My mother suggested it.» She looked around and saw that her mother had left the room. «She seems to enjoy stuffing him with sausages for breakfast.» She laughed.

«Irgendwas Neues?», fragte Manni.

«Nothing in particular – except that Sakina and Florian think they are on to a case of a disappearing quiz candidate. Crazy!»

«Was», rief Manni, «erzähl mal.»

«Oh it's nothing. I'll tell you tomorrow. By the way, do you have any new software you can bring over? Any new games? Beware of the X-ray machine at the airport, though. The strangest things can happen there.»

Chapter three

****

in which they find out something about dropping shots
und in dem Florian eine falsche Antwort gibt

Der *warm-up man* erzählte den Zuschauern dieselben Witze wie vor vier Wochen, als das erste Ausscheidungsspiel aufgenommen worden war. Auch nicht gerade der beste Job, dachte Florian, als Pausenclown das Publikum erst mal in Stimmung zu bringen und es dann später bei Laune zu halten, wenn was schief geht. Er trat von einem Bein auf das andere. Zehn Minuten standen sie jetzt schon in der Dekoration und warteten darauf, dass es endlich wirklich losging. Den ganzen Vormittag hatten sie mit Proben verbracht, wobei Rosemary, die junge Produktionsassistentin, an Stelle von Ginger Marley die Fragen gestellt hatte. Er wollte gerade etwas zu Una sagen, als der Aufnahmeleiter «Thirty seconds» rief. Also, gleich ging es los.

Florian atmete tief durch. Fünfzehn. Zehn. Fünf. Der *warm-up man* streckte beide Arme in die Luft: Publikum, sei bereit zum Klatschen, bedeutete das. Drei. Zwei. Eins. Die Eröffnungsfanfare. Die Stimme aus dem Off: «Ladies and Gentlemen, welcome your hostess, Ginger Marley.»

Der *warm-up man* schlug hoch über seinem Kopf die Hände zusammen. Das Publikum klatschte und johlte. Ginger Marley kam hinter der lila Pappkulisse hervor. «Thank you, thank you all very much.» Mit den Händen machte sie eine Bewegung, als wolle sie den Applaus dämpfen. Der *warm-up man* hörte auf zu klatschen, das Publikum hörte auf zu klatschen.

«Welcome to the eighth show of SUPERCHAIN – The Super European Quiz Show», wandte sie sich an das Fernsehpublikum. «We have reached the halfway mark now. During the last seven weeks you have seen seven teams winning their Qualifying Rounds, making it through to the quarterfinals.» Sie las jedes Wort von einer *cue-card* ab, von einem großen Plakat, das eine Assistentin direkt hinter der Kamera hochhielt. Auf dem Bildschirm sah es dann so aus, als würde sie alles frei in die Kamera sprechen.

«Let's take a quick look again at those winning teams. In Week One the Argonauts won against the Jugglers who are with us again today, because of all the losers they had the longest chain. In Week Two...»

«Stop», roared the floor-manager, «stop.»

Was ist denn nun schon wieder, dachte Florian. Joanne und Derek gingen zu den beiden Teams.

«Sorry about this, but they didn't blend in the video of the winner board in time», Derek explained.

«Does that mean the whole thing has to start from the beginning again?», Una wanted to know.

«I'm afraid so.»

Florians Gedanken schweiften ab. Fernsehen machen heißt warten können, hatte ihm Joanne bei der Aufnahme der ersten Sendung gleich am Anfang erklärt, und er hatte ihr nicht geglaubt. Aber es stimmte. Überhaupt war alles ziemlich kompliziert. Vor vier Wochen waren eine Woche lang die ersten sieben Sendungen aufgenommen worden, jeden Tag eine. Danach waren alle Kandidaten wieder nach Hause gefahren. Und jetzt ging es geballt wieder mit den Aufnahmen los – heute die Trostrunde, dann vier Viertelfinale, zwei Halbfinale und das Finale. Aber gezeigt wurde das Ganze über fünfzehn Wochen, einmal pro Woche, seit gestern. Im Fernsehen würde man erst in sechs Wochen sehen können, wie Maddy, Manni und Henk ihr Ausscheidungsspiel gewinnen, und dabei wurde morgen im Studio schon ihr Viertelfinale aufgenommen. Und auf dem Bildschirm sah es dann so aus, als wäre alles ganz aktuell und spontan. Hoffentlich überstehen wir diese Trostrunde, damit das nicht nur ein Kurzausflug nach London war ...

«Thirty seconds», unterbrach der Aufnahmeleiter seinen Gedankengang.

Dreißig, zwanzig, zehn, fünf, Fanfare, Klatschen, *Welcome*. Diesmal klappte die Einblendung der Tabelle, und Ginger erklärte, dass in den Viertelfinalen die Mannschaft, die ihr Ausscheidungsspiel mit der längsten Kette gewonnen hatte, gegen den Sieger dieser Trostrunde spiele, die Mannschaft mit der zweitlängsten Kette gegen die mit der siebtlängsten, die mit der dritt- und viertlängsten gegen die mit der sechst- und fünftlängsten. Und dann gehe es weiter wie bei einem Tennisturnier.

Auf dem Bildschirm war nun wieder Ginger zu sehen: «Today we have our Consolation Match where the two teams who had the longest chains of all the losing teams play against each other. Only one of them can go through to the quarterfinal. Let's now welcome them. A round of applause for the Jitterbugs – Yvonne from Bordeaux, Lasse from Helsinki and George from Birmingham.»

Wieder trieb der *warm-up man* das Publikum zu Begeisterungsstürmen.

«What have you got on your shirt, George?», Ginger Marley shrieked.

Auf dem Lacoste-Hemd von George war ein Mini-Käfig aus Holz zu sehen, den er sich aus Zahnstochern und Draht zusammengebastelt hatte.

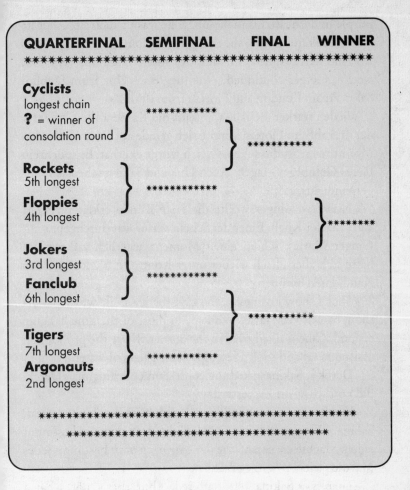

QUARTERFINAL	SEMIFINAL	FINAL	WINNER

Cyclists
longest chain
? = winner of
consolation round

Rockets
5th longest

Floppies
4th longest

Jokers
3rd longest

Fanclub
6th longest

Tigers
7th longest

Argonauts
2nd longest

«It stops the crocodile from running away», George told her.

«Oh, I see! How clever!»

«His shirt wouldn't be worth as much without the crocodile», whispered Sakina. Una was surprised. Sakina didn't usually make bitchy remarks. She looked at George. He blushed purple underneath his make-up. If he wasn't such a blusher he would look quite cute, she thought. Five out of ten.

«And here we have the unlucky losers from our very first week», Ginger continued, «the Jugglers – Una from Dublin, Sakina from London and Florian from Berlin.»

Wieder starker Beifall, während die Kamera die Gesichter der drei abfuhr. Florian konnte sich gerade auf einem der vielen Monitore im Studio sehen. Gleich wurde es ernst. Er spürte ein flaues Gefühl im Magen. Auch Una und Sakina sahen sehr angespannt aus.

«Now...» Ginger wollte die erste Runde erklären. Peng! Ein scharfer Knall. Einer der Scheinwerfer war durchgebrannt. Ginger Marley schien einen Moment ärgerlich zu werden, hatte sich aber gleich wieder unter Kontrolle. Sie kam zu den Kandidaten hinüber.

«That's show business», she gave them a smile which Sakina thought was very false, «you spend most of the time hanging around.» She walked over to the corner where the production assistants sat and took a few sips from a glass of water.

«Derek», Sakina asked the contestant coordinator, «Derek, did you see us on TV yesterday?»

«Yes, it came across really well, didn't it? You looked great, Sakina.» Florian mochte Derek nicht. Das sagt der bestimmt jedem, dachte er, genau wie der *warm-up man* bestimmt jedes Mal die gleichen Witze erzählt.

«Thanks», Sakina felt flattered, «but that's not what I wanted to ask you about. Remember Andy?»

«Of course I do», Derek nodded.

«Well, did you notice anything strange about him on TV yesterday?»

Derek thought for a while. «No», he said finally, «I can't

28

think of anything, why?» He looked like he didn't know what she was talking about.

«Well», Sakina paused, «the fellow on the television yesterday... I thought he looked a bit different from the Andy we met in the studio.»

Derek laughed. «But you were there when it was recorded», he insisted, «you saw him yourself. Sometimes people look a bit different on television – the make-up and all that.»

Sakina nodded but she wasn't satisfied.

«Okay, we have an edit point», the floor manager shouted, «stand by everyone. We'll come in again after the video of the winner board. Close-up of Ginger introducing the Consolation Match and the teams. No applause. Thirty seconds.»

Der *warm-up man* hielt den Zeigefinger vor die Lippen, das Mädchen mit den *cue cards* hinter der Kamera suchte den richtigen Text heraus, Ginger lächelte und ab ging es. Diesmal problemlos. Nach der Vorstellung der Teilnehmer fuhr Ginger fort:

«Just in case any of our viewers were away on holidays over the past few weeks, I'd better give you a quick rundown of the rules again. Whoever gets the most links of the Superchain is the winner. There are four Rounds and in each Round the links have to be got by different means. You'll see how as we move along. And now we'll start with Round I. Will you follow me contestants, please.»

Alle Lichter blinkten. Ginger Marley strich sich ihre Haare zurecht. Das konnte sie, denn auf dem Bildschirm sah man jetzt nur die Ketten blinken. Wie billig die ganze Dekoration aussieht, dachte Florian. Alles dicke Pappe. Und im Fernsehen wirkt das so toll.

In der ersten Runde gab es Fragen und Aufgaben aus drei

Bereichen: Wissen, Geschicklichkeit und Potpourri. Jede Mannschaft bestimmte selbst, wer welchen Bereich übernahm. Für die Jugglers war klar, dass Sakina für den Bereich Geschicklichkeit verantwortlich sein würde. Da war sie eindeutig besser als Una und Florian. Bei dem Spiel gegen die Argonauts hatte sich gezeigt, dass wie erwartet der Bereich Wissen nicht gerade Florians Stärke war, also übernahm Una in der ersten Runde dieses Ressort. Für Florian blieb das Potpourri übrig.

Ginger erklärte den Zuschauern, dass diese Runde aus vier Durchgängen bestand. In jedem Durchgang gab es für jede Mannschaft eine Wissensfrage, eine Geschicklichkeitsaufgabe und eine Aufgabe aus dem Bereich Potpourri. Das konnte alles Mögliche sein. Um ein Glied der Kette zum Leuchten zu bringen, musste eine Mannschaft dreimal hintereinander ihre Frage beziehungsweise Aufgabe korrekt lösen. Zweimal hintereinander richtig und dann eine falsch nützte einer Mannschaft nichts; da musste sie wieder von neuem beginnen.

«We have drawn lots and the Jugglers are going to begin», Ginger continued, «and they have decided that Una is going to be responsible for knowledge in this round, Sakina for the area of skill and the mixed bag tasks go to Florian. Now, let's see what they'll have to do», she finished.

Una watched the electronic display board nervously to find out what area she would have to answer questions on. Please don't let it be history, she thought. It was sport. Phew! That was lucky. And the first question was a lucky one for her, too. Ginger wanted to know the host country of the 1990 soccer World Cup. Italy, of course! It was the first time ever that Ireland had qualified for the World Cup so everybody in Ireland knew about the Italian venue – even those who weren't interested in soccer.

Sie sieht wahnsinnig gut aus, wie sie das macht, dachte Florian, als er Sakina bei ihrer Aufgabe zusah. Sie musste sechs Hüte auf einen Hutständer werfen, und mindestens drei mussten hängen bleiben.

«Well done, Sakina», Ginger Marley exclaimed, «now if Florian can do as well as you and Una, the Jugglers will have their first link of the day. Ready, Florian?»

Florian schluckte. Seine Aufgabe hieß ‹What happens next?›. Man sieht einen Filmausschnitt, der hält an einer bestimmten Stelle, und man muss raten, was als Nächstes passiert. Der Film lief ab.

Es war ein Ausschnitt aus einem James-Bond-Film. Eine schöne Frau in einem langen Wickelkleid, einer Art Sari, stand auf einem Balkon. Mit dem Rücken zur Straße. James Bond ging auf sie zu. «I don't know how to say good bye», sagte die Frau verführerisch. «Actions speak louder than words», antwortete James Bond und trat ganz nahe an sie heran. Leise, romantische Musik im Hintergrund. «You're so right», hauchte die Frau. James Bond... Der Film blieb bei einer Großaufnahme von Bonds Gesicht stehen. Was kann denn jetzt passieren, fragte sich Florian. Entweder küsst er sie oder er schmeißt sie vom Balkon, falls sie ein Feind ist. Oder vielleicht bricht auch der ganze Balkon zusammen. Keine Ahnung. «He is going to kiss her», entschied er sich.

«It looks like it, and it does happen in so many James Bond situations», antwortete Ginger, «but not this time, I'm afraid. Let's take a look at what happened. It's from the film ‹Octopussy›.»

Der Film lief weiter. Die Frau hatte offensichtlich vorher ein Ende ihres Saris am Balkon festgeknotet, jetzt kippte sie einfach rückwärts über den Balkon, ihr Sari wickelte sich auf und funktionierte als eine Art Fangleine. Sicher landete sie auf der Straße.

What a load of rubbish, thought Sakina when she saw it. «Sorry, Florian», Ginger said, «the Jugglers now have to start again to get three correct answers or tasks in a row to get a link of the chain.»

Blödmann, schimpfte sich Florian und sah zu den Jitterbugs hinüber. Lasse aus Helsinki hatte ein überlegenes Lächeln auf dem Gesicht, und George und Yvonne flüsterten sich etwas zu. Die freuen sich natürlich, dass wir das erste Glied der Kette nicht geschafft haben, dachte er. Freut euch bloß nicht zu früh.

Auch die Jitterbugs machten nicht alles richtig, und die Jugglers wurden im Verlauf der Runde besser. Drei Glieder der Kette hatten beide Mannschaften am Ende zum Leuchten gebracht. In der zweiten Runde behielten die Jugglers knapp die Nase vorn, in der dritten Runde waren die Jugglers eindeutig besser: 6 : 5 führten sie vor der letzten Runde, die nun die Entscheidung bringen musste. Florian und Una erledigten beide ihre erste Aufgabe richtig.

And Sakina answered a question on Kylie Minogue correctly, bringing the score up to seven links for the Jugglers while the Jitterbugs still only had five.

«Well done Jugglers», declared Ginger Marley, «that means the score is now seven to six.»

«No, it isn't», Una protested.

«Stimmt doch gar nicht», entfuhr es Florian fast gleichzeitig.

«Hey, wait a minute», Sakina cried, «the Jitterbugs only have five links.»

«Stop, everyone, stop», the floor manager walked over onto the set. Ginger Marley put her eyes up to heaven. The cameramen stood behind their cameras and relaxed.

«Look kids», the floor manager said to both teams, «if Ginger makes a mistake like that, just pretend nothing has happened. We can continue recording and when we are finished we can do a retake of her giving the score she should have given when she made the mistake. Then we can drop that shot into the video tape later when we are editing.»

Florian verstand nur Bahnhof. Das heißt, eigentlich nicht, denn er verstand die meisten Wörter, aber sie schienen keinen Sinn zu ergeben. Joanne kam zu ihm herüber.

«Verrückt, nicht?», sagte sie. «Aber es stimmt tatsächlich. Die, die da oben über dem Studio sitzen, der Regisseur und die Leute, die für Ton und Bild zuständig sind, können einzelne Bilder oder Wörter nachträglich einblenden. Es ist billiger, wenn wir erst mal weiterdrehen und hinterher was ändern, als wenn wir dauernd unterbrechen. Es sei denn, es ist etwas, was Folgen für den weiteren Ablauf hat. Dann müssen wir natürlich unterbrechen. Okay?» Sie sah Florian fragend an.

«Okay», nickte er, aber irgendwie gefiel ihm das nicht. Dann könnte man ja alles nachträglich verändern.

«So you see», the floor manager continued, «if you shout something like ‹it's a mistake› we have to stop the recording altogether. If it happens again, just stay calm. The people upstairs will stop the show if the mistake can't be repaired with retakes and editing.»

While waiting for the recording to start again, Ginger Marley spoke to her young contestants. Sakina asked her a question. «If you can drop in shots like that, when you are editing the tape, then it would be possible to take one of us out of this recording and put someone else in instead, wouldn't it?»

«What a strange idea», Ginger Marley laughed, «but yes, I suppose it would be technically possible. Expensive, though, with all the retakes. And I would have to be there so that the transitions between the ‹someone else› and me could be retaken, too.» She looked Sakina straight in the eye. «Had you someone in mind?»

Florian wollte ihr einen warnenden Blick zuwerfen.

Mensch, Sakina, wenn der Andy wirklich ausgetauscht worden ist, dann war Ginger bestimmt dabei. Also hat es auch keinen Zweck, ihr zu verraten, was wir wissen oder vermuten. Aber Sakina fing Florians Blick nicht auf.

«Well», Sakina hesitated a second, «I thought the Andy we saw on the television yesterday wasn't the same one who was in the studio when the show was recorded.»

Ginger Marley laughed loudly. «What a funny girl! No, if we had done something like that I would have had to spend time doing the retakes and I have been fully booked out for weeks. Your eyes must have been playing tricks on you. And anyway, why on earth would we want to go to the expense of doing something silly like that?»

«Stand by everyone», the floor manager called, «we're ready for the retake. Sakina, you say *Kylie Minogue* again, the audience claps, and the score is seven five, okay? Ready to roll.»

Während Sakina ihre Antwort wiederholte, überlegte Florian. Wenn man jemand technisch auswechseln kann, hatte Sakina dann vielleicht doch Recht? Das laute Lachen von Ginger Marley hatte doch sehr falsch geklungen.

Viertes Kapitel

****

*in dem Manni einen Zeichen-Trick findet
and in which Maddy grows wings*

The doorbell rang. «We are the champions, we are the champions», Maddy heard them singing on the doorstep before she opened the door. Florian was standing there in the middle with his arms around Una and Sakina on either side.

«You did it!», Maddy shouted and embraced all three of them. «Come in, champs – even if it is only champs of the Consolation Match. «Now this», she said pointing to herself, «is what a real champion looks like. The Floppies will win the final, even if we have to beat you to do so.»

«Das woll'n wir mal sehen», sagte Florian, während sie ins Wohnzimmer gingen, «ihr müsst morgen erst mal euer Viertelfinale gewinnen. Da bin ich...»

«No German», Una interrupted him.

«Oh sorry, I mean...»

«It doesn't matter what you mean.» Now it was Maddy who interrupted him. She turned to Una and Sakina: «Tell me about your victory today.»

«Easy as pie», Una boasted, «we had...» She didn't get any further because the doorbell rang.

Maddy went to open the door. «Manni! It's great to see you again», she said when she saw him standing there.

They gave each other a big hug.

«Mensch, Maddy, toll!»

«Hello, Maddy», said a quiet voice.

«Oh Henk, hello.» She gave him a kiss on the cheek. In doing so, she somehow managed to knock against his glasses. They fell off his nose but Henk managed to catch them akwardly before they hit the floor.

«Sorry», he said, looking very embarrassed.

«No, I'm sorry», insisted Maddy, «it was my fault.» There was a moment's silence. Then she said: «Come on in, today's winners have just arrived as well.»

Im Wohnzimmer gab es ein großes Hallo. Henk kannte Sakina, Florian und Una noch nicht, und auch Manni und Una trafen sich zum ersten Mal. Six out of ten, thought Una taking a good look at Manni. This could be an interesting quiz.

Florian, Una und Sakina berichteten ausführlich von ihrem Trostrundensieg über die Jitterbugs.

Mein Gott, mit was für einem Tempo Una Englisch spricht, dachte Manni, da kommt man ja wirklich kaum mit. Sie erzählte gerade, wie der Lasse von den Jitterbugs vor dem Schminken ausgesehen hatte – lauter Pickel im Gesicht, wie ein Streuselkuchen – und wie er nach dem *make-up* plötzlich ganz glatt und schön ausgesehen hatte.

«I'm telling you, if that's what make-up can do for some people then I think I should be looking at it more seriously», she said.

«Yuk. I can't stand the stuff. I'm sure it gives you pimples, covering your face with that muck», was Sakina's response.

«Well, you would say that, wouldn't you», said Una. She was getting tired with the way everyone reacted to her teammate in the studio. Okay, so she was fantastic-looking, but some people – like Una herself – had much more sparkling personalities. At least that's what she thought. «But even with the pimples removed I wouldn't have touched that Lasse with a barge-pole», she continued. «He was wearing an acrylic jumper. Imagine! Yukki, yuk, yuk. Acrylic jumpers are absolutely out, but obviously the news hasn't reached wherever it is he comes from yet.»

«Helsinki», Sakina said.

Eh, mal langsam, dachte Florian. Wir wollen schließlich ein Quiz gewinnen. Warum war da bloß so eine Spannung zwischen den beiden?

«Anyway», Sakina continued, «I don't think it's that important how people look. You talk about appearances all the time and give fellows marks out of ten for the way they look. How would you like if people did the same to you?»

Una raised her eyebrows and shrugged her shoulders. She was blushing slightly. «I wouldn't mind.»

Manni wusste zwar nicht, warum, aber er merkte, dass die beiden nicht besonders gut aufeinander zu sprechen waren. Schnell versuchte er, das Thema zu wechseln.

«Wir müssen erst mal euern Sieg feiern», schlug er vor, «und zwar schnell, denn Derek – der hat uns vorhin vom Hotel hierher gefahren – holt uns in zwei Stunden wieder ab. Der hat wohl Angst, dass ihm die Kandidaten für morgen verloren gehen.»

Una made an impatient noise with her tongue and raised her eyes to heaven. «Have you ever thought for one moment that there are people around who don't speak your language?», she said to Manni, then turning to Henk added «I hope at least you won't be making that awful noise.»

«I'm afraid I do understand it and I speak a little, too.» Henk blushed. He poked at his glasses with his finger, pushing them up onto the bridge of his nose.

«And he speaks French as well», Maddy commented.

«And Dutch», Henk said quietly.

O wei, dachte Manni, da habe ich wohl offensichtlich nicht die richtige Art gewählt, Una zu besänftigen.

«Oh God, so that means I'm the only Kraut-free zone, does it?», Una complained. «Well you aren't the only ones who can speak funny languages. Get an earful of this. *Go mbeith páiste gach blian agat.* I'll bet none of you got that!»

Was hatte sie gesagt? ‹Gomeh poschte gach bli en agat› oder so ähnlich. Florian war ganz durcheinander.

«What does it mean?», Sakina asked, wondering if she should join in this ridiculous language competition by saying something in her mother tongue.

«It's the Irish for: ‹May you have a child every year», said Una proudly. «It is a toast, you know, before you take a drink.»

«Talking about drink… when are we going to drink to to-day's winners?», sagte Manni schnell, denn er wollte dieser Una zeigen, dass er auch auf Englisch gut drauf war. Wirklich ganz schön kess war die. Er sah sie direkt an. Sie wich nicht aus, sondern erwiderte seinen Blick.

It was Maddy who interrupted their staring match. «Any new software for me, Manni?», she asked.

«Yes, a detective game, very, äh very, passend.»

«Suitable?»

«Yeah, it's called *The Missing Link*.»

«As long as we don't miss any links tomorrow», Maddy said.

«Oh», erinnerte sich Manni plötzlich, «on the phone this morning you said something about Florian and Sakina chasing a missing person.»

Das Stichwort war gefallen. Sakina und Florian erzählten jetzt von ihrem Verdacht und von ihren ersten fehlgeschlagenen Versuchen, was rauszukriegen.

«And I am still convinced that something is wrong», Sakina said finally, «that Ginger Marley woman with her smile as sweet as sugar and her huge laugh! I think they are covering up something.»

«But what, and more important, why? It doesn't make sense», Una declared.

«Ehm», Henk cleared his throat. He had been silent up till now. «Well, if you are right and they did something like that then of course they won't tell you anything. After all, you were there when the first recording happened. But maybe Maddy, Manni and I can find out a bit more about how and why it could have been done. As far as the people in the studio are concerned we are just another team and have nothing to do with you. So we could ask questions about the technology of it all and it shouldn't sound suspicious.» He took a deep breath and blushed.

The poor fellow, thought Una, he probably hasn't said as much as that for a long time. He looks so shy. And all his blushing! But he was okay. She upped his rating from two to three out of ten.

Keine schlechte Idee von Henk, dachte Florian, und schließlich müssen die Argonauts ja auch noch ihr Viertelfinale spielen, da finden wir bestimmt mehr raus. Aber die – wer immer das war – wissen natürlich schon, dass wir was miteinander zu tun haben. Ich wohne bei Maddy, und Henk und Manni waren gerade hierher gefahren worden. Er erzählte den anderen von seinen Bedenken.

«True», Maddy replied, «but maybe not all of them know. Let's try it anyway.»

Es klingelte. Es war schon Derek, der Manni und Henk abholen kam. Die zwei Stunden waren mit all dem Erzählen sehr schnell vergangen. Sakina and Una also left with Derek. He was going drop Sakina home and give Una a lift to her aunt's.

Maddy yawned. «I suppose I should go to bed now if I want to be fresh for our quarterfinal tomorrow», she said to Florian. «Good night.»

«Träum schön», sagte er, «und wie heißt nochmal die Hauptstadt von Rumänien?»

Manni, Henk und Maddy hatten zwar gesagt, sie würden nach etwas Verdächtigem ausschauen, aber sie hatten nicht die geringste Ahnung, wonach sie eigentlich suchen sollten, und außerdem verlangte ihr Viertelfinale gegen die Rockets, ein Team aus Swansea, Lyon und St. Johann in Tirol, ihre gesamte Aufmerksamkeit.

Manni merkte, wie ihn die Kameras, Scheinwerfer, die Computer und Anzeigetafeln, wie ihn die ganze Atmosphäre gefangen nahm.

Maddy had the first general knowledge question, and sport was the category which the light on the electronic display board chose for her.

«And now a sports question for Maddy. Can you tell me when and where Judo was first included in Olympic Games competition?»

«In Tokyo in 1964», Maddy had no problem with that one. As Ginger Marley was saying «Well done», one of the assistants on the floor was waving a cue-card at her, pointing energetically at the third line.

«Of course if I remember rightly, judo was one of your hobbies, wasn't it Maddy? What a lucky coincidence!», she said,

```
MADDY BUTLER
    LONDON
Hobbies:  JUDO
          COMPUTERS
          PEN FRIENDS

WANTS TO WORK WITH COMPUTERS
       AND TRAVEL
```

flashing one of her widest smiles. Today's lip colour was cherry.

Auch Manni und Henk konnten ihre Aufgaben lösen. Das erste Glied der Kette war da. Es lief blendend in dieser ersten Runde: Sie schafften alle vier möglichen Glieder. Aber die Rockets waren auch nicht schlecht und so stand es nach der ersten Runde 4 : 3. Nach einer kurzen Pause ging es mit der Aufnahme der zweiten Runde weiter.

«It's up to each team now to say who is to do what», Ginger Marley reminded the teams. «One of you will be given the title of a film, he or she will have to mime it to another member of the team who will have to draw it for the third. The last one then has to name the film.»

Maddy remembered the conversation they had the first time they had had to decide who would do what. «How good are you at miming?», she had asked Henk although she couldn't imagine that he was very good. He was probably too shy to let himself go properly. Henk had blushed. «Not very good, I'm afraid. And before you ask, my drawing isn't any better.»

«Well, I suppose being a wizard at general knowledge is good enough. What about you, Manni? What are you best at?»

«Schlechter Schauspieler. Mittelmäßiger Zeichner», hatte er geantwortet.

«I'll mime then, Manni will have to guess and draw and Henk will have to give the answer from Manni's picture», Maddy had decided. And they agreed to stick to that combination after that.

Die Rockets hatten auch bestimmt, wer schauspielern, zeichnen und raten musste. Diese Runde erforderte einige Vorbereitungen. Als erstes kam eine Trennwand aus dem Boden, sodass keine Mannschaft sehen konnte, was die andere machte. Dann wurden den beiden, die die Zeichnung erraten sollten, Henk und Erika, das Mädchen aus Österreich, die Augen verbunden, damit sie nichts von der Pantomime mitkriegen konnten. Außerdem bekamen sie und die beiden Zeichner Kopfhörer auf, sodass sie nichts hören konnten. Der *warm-up man* unterhielt während dieser Vorbereitung das Publikum mit Witzen.

«Alright, teams, are you ready? Yes? Good. Then Maddy from London and Sheila from Swansea, come over to me now and I'll tell you the title of the film you are to mime.»

Manni schaute zu, wie Ginger Marley den Mädchen eine Karte zeigte, auf der offensichtlich der Titel stand. Beide zogen sofort eine Grimasse: wie stellt man das bloß dar?

Maddy ran back to her side of the partition. She thought for a few seconds. Then she held up six fingers.

«Six?», sagte Manni zögernd. «The Six?... Is the word six in the title?»

Maddy shook her head. She held up one finger, then two, then three, then four...

Zählen kann ich auch, Mädchen, dachte Manni, was meinte sie bloß damit? «Six, six … aha, are there six words in the title?»

Maddy's face broke into a smile and she nodded furiously. She held up one finger and then two.

«The second word?», fragte Manni und sah, wie Maddy nickte.

Maddy started to run around the studio floor in circles, waving her arms up and down by her side like a bird. At least she thought it should look like a bird.

So was Verrücktes, das sagt mir gar nichts. Was soll das bloß, dachte Manni. Schnell ratterte er alle möglichen Bewegungs-arten durch. Ballett vielleicht?

Maddy's face dropped when Manni said ‹ballet›. Is he stupid or am I doing the wrong thing, she wondered. Still she continued to run around flapping her arms.

«Dance?» Anscheinend nicht.

«Bird?»

She paused for a moment and thought about it.

«Bird?», versuchte es Manni nochmal, hoffnungsvoll.

Maddy screwed up her face and shook her head slowly to show that he wasn't right but he was close. She moved both her hands around in circles between Manni and herself as if she wanted to pull some more information from him.

«It's not birds, it's …» Wieder machte Maddy die schlagende Bewegung mit den Armen. «Wings!», platzte es aus Manni heraus.

Maddy wedelte mit der Hand – nicht richtig, aber auch nicht falsch, hieß das wohl, interpretierte Manni.

Flap, flap, she went again with her arms. It must be obvious, she thought. She heard the audience laugh and clap. Are they laughing at us or at the others?

43

«Bird... wings... fly?» Manni war fast am Verzweifeln, aber endlich zeigte Maddys Gesicht, dass er richtig geraten hatte. Aber offensichtlich nicht ganz richtig. Sofort nachdem sie heftig genickt hatte, machte sie wieder diese ‹So-lala›-Bewegung mit der Hand. Also *fly* war vielleicht nicht ganz richtig, aber er war nahe dran. Jetzt zeigte sie mit ihrem Daumen über ihre Schulter nach hinten.

Past tense, Manni, come one, she urged him in her thoughts.

«Fly... in the past.»

Heftiges Nicken von Maddy.

«Flied!»

Heftiges Kopfschütteln.

«Fly, flowed?»

Auch nicht.

O Gott, dachte Manni, das darf doch nicht an einem blöden unregelmäßigen Verb scheitern! Was gab es denn für Filme mit der Vergangenheit von ‹fliegen›?

Maddy sneezed. And sneezed again. And coughed.

Was soll das nun auf einmal sein? Niesen? Husten? Erkältung? Grippe? – *Flu*! Natürlich! *Fly – flew*. Also, das zweite Wort des Filmtitels hieß *flew*.

Maddy nodded and held one finger up. This could be very difficult, she thought.

«The first word», sagte Manni. Maddy nickte.

She held one finger up again.

«I know it's the first word», sagte er leicht gereizt. Wieder nickte sie und hielt zum dritten Mal einen Finger hoch. Einen Moment war Manni völlig ratlos, dann kam eine Idee:

«Has the word got something to do with ‹one›?»

Maddy nodded as furiously as she could.

«Is it the word ‹one›?», fragte Manni erstaunt.

Yes, nodded Maddy.

«One flew...» Er überlegte. «One flew over the cuckoo's nest?»

«Yes», Maddy shrieked. She was exhausted.

Manni konnte jetzt seinen Kopfhörer abnehmen. Derek befreite gerade Henk von den Augenklappen. Manni hätte zu gern gewusst, wie weit die andere Mannschaft war, aber alle Monitore waren in dieser Runde umgedreht. Dem Gelächter des Publikums nach waren sie auch noch nicht weit. Wie zeichne ich das bloß, dachte er, während Henk ihn erwartungsvoll ansah. Er fing mit dem Nest an.

«Is it a hat?», fragte Henk nach ein paar Strichen. Wie zeichnet man denn ein Nest, verdammt nochmal? Manni wurde ganz hektisch. Bloß nicht die Nerven verlieren. Er versuchte es mit einem Baum, der nicht sehr nach einem Baum aussah, aber der schien Henk zu reichen. «A tree!»

Gut. Er zeichnete einen Pfeil, der auf den Baum wies, und zeigte wieder auf das Nest. Komm, dachte er, im Baum gibt's keine Hüte. Also Junge, was ist das?

«A nest!» Henk hatte es begriffen.

Echt genial, lobte sich Manni, als er auf die Idee kam, nicht einen Vogel in das Nest zu setzen – wie würde Henk jemals auf einen Kuckuck kommen? –, sondern eine Kuckucksuhr hineinzulegen. Und schlecht sah sie auch nicht aus. Das isses, dachte er. Komm Henk, dachte Manni, mach alles klar.

«Clock!», said Henk with a smile on his face. He thought that was the answer. But he saw Manni's face drop. He had to keep guessing.

«A clock in the nest?»

Kopfschütteln.

45

«Time in the nest?»

Verzweifeltes Kopfschütteln.

«Nest time?»

Maddy thought Manni looked as if his eyes were going to pop out of his head with frustration. Manni zeigte immer wieder auf den kleinen Kuckuck.

«Cuckoo?»

Ja, ja, weiter, Henk, weiter, raste es durch Mannis Gehirn.

«Cuckoo's nest? Cuckoo's nest!»

Manni nickte. Richtig geraten. Aber offenbar kam Henk nicht von alleine auf den ganzen Teil. Also musste Manni weiterzeichnen. Wie zeichnet man bloß ‹One flew over…›?

Maddy was glad that she wasn't the person who had to draw. What would Manni do now? He was drawing furiously.

46

Er zeichnete zuerst eine Eins, die über dem Nest schwebte, dann verpasste er ihr noch ein Paar Flügel.

Henk's face lit up. «One flew over the cuckoo's nest!»

Maddy und Manni liefen auf ihn zu und klopften ihm auf die Schulter. «Well done, well done», the winning music was playing and Ginger Marley was congratulating the Floppies.

«Great», the floor manager said, «everybody has been very good. Thank you. We'll take a coffee break now and continue with Round 3 in forty minutes.»

Sie gingen zur Kantine. Manni, Maddy und Henk saßen zusammen mit Derek. «God, that was exhausting», Maddy exclaimed, «it felt like it went on forever. It must have taken ages.» Derek smiled. «It took just under three minutes from your first flapping of wings to Henk's correct guessing of the title. Not a minute longer.»

«Only three minutes?», rief Manni. «Ich dachte auch, äh, I thought it took much longer.»

«It's all so complicated, Derek», Maddy said, «with all these different rounds with different questions and tasks. And on top of that you have different teams from different countries playing each other on different days. How do you keep track of it all?»

«Oh, we have everyone and everything organized in our computer», Derek explained proudly. «I'd be lost without it.»

Manni kam eine Idee. Er sah Maddy an. War ihr das auch eingefallen? Aber sie schien restlos mit ihrem Eis beschäftigt.

«Everything, that is, except of course the questions», Derek went on, «because you never know what might...» He stared at Henk. «Christ almighty, Henk! Are you okay?» He rushed over to him. Blood was pouring out of Henk's nose. «I'll have to take you to the first aid station.»

«Thanks», Henk could be heard muttering through his bloody handkerchief.

«Will the two of you be alright by yourselves?», Derek asked over his shoulder as he was leaving the room. Maddy and Manni nodded their heads.

Sobald Derek und Henk außer Sicht waren, sprangen Maddy und Manni auf.

«And now to find the computer.» Maddy led the way.

Chapter five

****

*in which Henk makes it possible for Maddy and
Manni to continue their investigations
und in dem Manni mit einem fremden Computer spielt*

Auch Maddy war beim Stichwort Computer sofort klar geworden, dass sie in dem Computer was über den vertauschten Andy finden könnten. Aber sie hatte keine Miene verzogen. Ganz schön cool, dachte Manni voller Anerkennung. Solange Derek auf sie aufpasste, konnten sie nichts machen. Aber den hatte der Zufall in Gestalt von Henks Nasenbluten erst mal aus dem Verkehr gezogen. Sie liefen zurück ins Studio. Es war ganz leer. Gespenstisch sah es aus. Die grellen Lichter leuchteten nicht, es gab nur eine Art Notbeleuchtung und der Zuschauerraum war völlig verlassen. Die Pappkulisse sah noch billiger aus als während der Aufnahmen, so als ob man sie leicht umkippen könnte. Die Kameras standen unbemannt herum.

«Mensch, pass auf!», sagte Manni und fing Maddy, die gerade stolperte, auf.

«Bloody cable spaghetti», she grumbled. The floor was covered with hundreds of different cables, all different colours, all running in different directions.

Manni and Maddy were heading towards the production assistants' corner. The only computer they had seen so far was there in the studio. They knew it kept the score and lit up the link when the teams were playing. Did it also contain information about the teams?

49

Manni schaltete ihn an.

«Call up the directory», Maddy suggested.

Sie suchten nach etwas, das vielleicht ‹Contestants› oder ‹Teams› oder so ähnlich hieß. Fehlanzeige. Keiner der Namen der Dateien hörte sich so an, als ob er interessant sein und weiterführen konnte. Auch hieß keine Datei so wie eine der vierzehn Mannschaften. Was nun?

«We're not getting any further here. We'll have to find another computer», Maddy decided. «But where?» She tried to remember if she had ever seen Derek or Joanne sitting at one, but she thought not.

«Well, if it isn't two of the Floppies!» That was Rosemary, the production assistant who asked the questions during the rehearsals. Maddy's heart stopped beating for a second. Why hadn't they heard her coming?

«That's right», sagte Manni freundlich. Bloß nicht aussehen, als ob wir bei irgendetwas ertappt worden sind.

«Where's your nanny, then?», the production assistant wanted to know.

«Our what? Oh you mean Derek», said Maddy. So that was what they called the contestant coordinators. Nannies! As if they looked after babies. Honestly!

«He'll be back in a second. Someone called him away. He was just showing us the computer here. It's very interesting.» Manni lächelte freundlich. Würde sie ihnen das abkaufen?

Maddy joined in. «He had finished showing us, actually. Maybe we should go back and wait for him in the contestants' room.»

The production assistant frowned. «He should ask me in future if he wants to go showing you around my computer. You tell him that from me.»

«We will», sagte Manni mit einem unschuldigen Blick.

«Phew, that was close. I hope she doesn't mention it to Derek. Then we'll be in a right mess», Maddy commented when they got back to the contestants' room. Dieses Zimmer lag zwischen der Garderobe und dem *make-up*-Raum. Im Augenblick war niemand da. Nett eingerichtet war es, mit Sofas und bequemen Sesseln, in denen man sich ausruhen konnte. Außerdem gab es noch einen Riesenfernseher.

Manni zeigte auf die zweite Tür im Zimmer. «Weißt du eigentlich, was hinter der Tür da ist?», fragte er Maddy. Maddy looked at it. «It probably leads into the dressing room», she said, getting up and walking over to it. It wasn't locked. She opened the door. Then she turned around to Manni with a smile on her face: «Come and see for yourself!»

«Na bitte. Da ist er doch, unser Computer», sagte er erstaunt. Hinter der Tür war ein kleines Büro. Ein ganz kleines – es war wohl ursprünglich als Abstellkammer gedacht und wurde später dann als Mini-Büro verwendet. Darin befanden sich ein Stuhl und zwei Tische – ein ganz kleiner, auf dem ein Fernseher stand, und ein etwas größerer. Auf dem hatten eine Kaffeemaschine, ein Kaktus, ein Telefon und, wie Manni soeben bemerkte, ein Computer Platz. Das musste das Büro der *contestant coordinators* sein. Manni schaltete den Computer an.

Suddenly they heard footsteps approaching.

Manni wurde ganz blass. Sie zogen die Tür zu dem kleinen Büro zu. Gleichzeitig machte jemand die Tür zum *contestants' room* auf.

«Derek? Joanne?», hörten Manni und Maddy jemand rufen. «Where are they for God's sake?», hörten sie noch, bevor die Tür zugeschlagen wurde.

«We'd better hurry», said Maddy. Her stomach was in knots. I don't think I am cut out for this sort of thing at all, she thought.

Manni hatte inzwischen gesehen, dass das Datenbanksystem dBase auf der Festplatte war und dass es eine Datei mit dem Namen ‹Contest.dbf› gab.

«You know your way around dBase, don't you?», Maddy asked. «I have a copy of one of the early versions at home but I'm a bit rusty.»

«It's easy with the menu in the newer versions», antwortete er, «you'll see.» Er gab den DISPLAY-Befehl, baute einen Suchbefehl für ‹Manni› auf und schickte ihn ab.

Auf dem Bildschirm waren auf einmal viele Informationen über ihn zu sehen. Name, Adresse, Telefonnummer, Staatsangehörigkeit, zu welcher Mannschaft er gehörte, seine Hobbys, was er werden wollte – alles Details, die er auf dem Teilnehmerformular angegeben hatte. Außerdem waren dort auch seine Flugtermine zu lesen – Ankunft in und Abflug von London – und wo er in London untergebracht war.

«That's exactly the file we were looking for!», exclaimed Maddy, «now let's see what Andy's details are.»

Just as she said that, they heard the door to the contestants' room being opened once again. Maddy quickly left the little office and closed the door behind her. It was Derek and Henk.

«Oh Henk!», Maddy cried and ran to put her arms around him as if he had just come back from the war, «are you okay?» She knew she was being overdramatic, but she got such a fright when she saw them come into the room that she had to do something to cover it up.

Henk blushed purple and looked very embarrassed.

Manni in dem kleinen Zimmer wagte kaum zu atmen. Hoffentlich kann sie Derek ablenken, dachte er, sonst stehen wir ganz schön dumm da. Und bloß keine Taste des Computers berühren, sonst produziert der noch ein Geräusch.

«Easy on there Maddy», Derek came to Henk's protection, «it was only a nosebleed. It stopped shortly after we got to the first aid room but the nurse kept him lying down there for a moment anyway.» He looked around the room. «Where's Manni?», he asked. «Manni?», she echoed, thinking fast.

«Yes Manni. Remember, your friend and team-mate?»

«Don't be silly, of course I do. He's gone... he's gone to the toilet», she answered. «Got the collywobbles. He always does before recording. He said not to wait for him here, he'll join us on the set.»

Derek looked at his watch. «Okay. I suppose we'd better get a move on. We're due there now. Are you okay, Henk?»

Henk nodded.

Manni schaffte es gerade noch rechtzeitig, zurückzukommen, bevor es weiterging. Maddy und Henk sahen ihn fragend an. Er machte eine ganz kleine Bewegung mit den Händen: zwei Fäuste mit hochgestrecktem Daumen. Er hatte es geschafft.

Round 3 was the ‹true or false› round. Both teams were given a statement and then each contestant had to press a button – the ‹true› button if they thought the statement was true, the ‹false› button if they thought it wasn't. The trick in this round was that a team only got a link if all three members had pressed the same button and their answer was correct. If they all pressed the same button and it was wrong, then they would lose a link. The contestants couldn't talk to or look at one another while the statements were being read, and they couldn't see which buttons the others were pressing.

«Ready, teams?», Ginger Marley asked. «Here comes the first statement: You are standing in a room with white walls. Two spotlights are shining on you from different angles, a white one and a red one. There will be two shadows on the wall, one red and one black one. True or false?»

True – True – False. Manni, Maddy, Henk. Stupid Henk, Maddy cursed. That's our link gone. And the Rockets had three ‹trues›.

«Henk, you are odd one out here», said Ginger Marley, «but you are the only one who is right. It is false. Do you know what the correct answer is?»

«Red and green», said Henk without hesitating.

«Well done», Ginger Marley said, «pity I can't give you a link for that answer but the Floppies don't get a link this time and the Rockets even have to lose one.

Manni fand, dass er nicht so richtig bei der Sache war. Gut, dass diese Runde sowieso nur ein erweitertes Glücksspiel war. Bei zwei der drei nächsten Fragen hatten sie mehr Glück: Alle drei hatten Recht mit ihrer Antwort, dass Argentinien 1958 nicht Fußballweltmeister geworden war, und es stimmte, dass die Hälfte aller elfjährigen Jungen und ein Drittel aller elfjährigen Mädchen in Großbritannien mindestens einmal pro Woche Alkohol tranken. Maddy breathed a sigh of relief. They were well in the lead.

«Break. Candidates back here in twenty minutes for the last round», the floor manager announced. Maddy, Henk and Manni tried to find a corner where they could be alone. «True or false: there are two Andys», Maddy joked. Bevor Manni antworten konnte, mischte sich Henk ein.

«Bei all den Mikrophonen und Leuten hier sollten wir lieber deutsch reden – das ist sicherer.»

Maddy nodded. Not only did he know about coloured shadows and happened to have a nosebleed at the right moment, he was thinking alone the right lines as well.

She quickly told him what she and Manni had done while Derek was looking after him. Henk didn't seem to be too surprised.

«Also, ich hab die Adresse von Andy aus dem Computer rausgeholt und aufgeschrieben. Hier. Andy Hedley heißt er.» Manni kramte einen Zettel aus der Tasche und zeigte ihn ihnen.

«And how will we know whether it's the real Andy... äh woher wissen wir...?», Maddy asked.

Manni unterbrach sie: «Tja, das weiß ich auch nicht. Der Suchbefehl hat nur einen Andy ausfindig gemacht. Ein zweiter war nicht drin.»

«Klar, wenn sie die beiden Andys ausgetauscht haben, dann haben sie natürlich auch die Daten im Computer geändert», sagte Henk.

«Logisch. Das heißt, dass dies die Daten vom falschen Andy sind. Immerhin könnte man versuchen, über den was rauszukriegen. Aber wo finden wir die von dem richtigen?», fragte Manni.

«Well, well, is there a secret meeting going on here, or what?», Derek interrupted them. «Do you want to join me for a cup of something?»

«No thanks», Maddy said, «we just want to decide on a strategy for the last round.»

«Okay, I'll leave you to it, then.» Derek turned to Henk and asked: «Nose alright again, Henk?» Henk nodded.

«Gut, dass wir deutsch gesprochen haben», atmete Manni auf, als Derek gegangen war. «Wir haben sowieso echt Glück heute.

Vor allem, dass deine Nase gerade angefangen hat zu bluten, als wir Derek loswerden wollten.»

«Glück?!», erwiderte Henk. «Das war Absicht!»

«Was!» – «What!», kam es erstaunt von Manni und Maddy zurück. «Absicht?»

«Ja, wenn ich mich voll darauf konzentriere, kann ich Nasenbluten haben, einfach so.» Er wurde leicht rot. «Ich mach das oft vor dem Sportunterricht, besonders im Winter, wenn wir Geräteturnen machen sollen.»

Maddy was fascinated. She had never heard anything like this before. Henk rose instantly in her estimation. Up until a few weeks ago he had just been a pen friend with whom she exchanged computer programs and letters about computers, but she hadn't really known an awful lot about him. She had met him for the first time when they had played their Qualifying Round and she hadn't been very impressed by him, even though he had answered a lot of questions correctly. But now it was clear that he had thought along exactly the same lines as she and Manni at lunchtime and had reacted brilliantly. Faking a nosebleed! «I don't believe it», she said.

Henk looked slightly insulted. «I can show you if you don't believe me», he offered.

«Oh God no!», she shrieked. «I didn't really mean I didn't believe it – it's just a way of saying…»

«Es ist unglaublich, unwahrscheinlich», warf Manni ein.

«Genau», Maddy nodded.

«Bei dBase gibt es keine automatischen ‹back-up-Dateien›, wenn ich mich nicht irre», wechselte Manni das Thema, «sonst könnte man mal sehen, ob sie in einer alten Fassung der Datei noch den anderen Andy haben.»

«Vielleicht haben sie aber noch irgendwo eine alte Diskette, auf der sie ihre Daten… hmm… up-gebacked… gebackuped… oder wie auch immer… haben», überlegte Henk.

Maddy could have thrown her arms around him. «Of course, there was…» She interrupted herself. «Na klar, da stand eine Kiste mit Disketten neben dem Computer.» She looked at her watch. «Wir haben nicht mehr genug Zeit, aber vielleicht gibt es ja wieder eine Unterbrechung.» She flashed a smile at Henk.

«Und ich werde mich sehr beeilen», sagte Manni.

Just then Joanne walked over towards them. «Wobei wirst du dich beeilen?», fragte sie.

«Bei meiner nächsten Geschicklichkeitsaufgabe», erklärte er.

Die letzte Runde. Mit einem furiosen Start gewannen die Rockets zwei Glieder in der Kette, während bei den Floppies alles schief lief. Es schien, als seien sie nicht mit voller Konzentration bei der Sache. Dann passierte es. Gerade als die Kamera in Großaufnahme zeigte, wie Henk seiner *general-knowledge*-Frage zuhörte, begann Blut aus seiner Nase zu laufen.

«Uuaagh», kreischte eine Produktionsassistentin.

«Oh my God, Henk, what's happened?» Joanne shouted and ran over to him.

«Stop», roared the floor manager to his crew.

Manni wollte gerade ein paar Schritte in Richtung Ausgang machen, als Joanne ihn am Arm zog: «Komm mit, wir bringen Henk erst mal aus dem Studio.» Manni blieb nichts anderes übrig, er musste mit. Hilfe suchend schaute er sich zu Maddy um. Die zuckte mit den Achseln.

Maddy looked around. Everybody was busy either looking after Henk or else getting the video tape and the studio ready to pick up the recording again at the right spot. She would have to do it herself. Would she remember how to cope with dBase? The menu was easy but what about the search condition? She had no choice. She looked around again. Derek was flirting with one of the production assistants. Nobody was paying any attention to her. She slipped out of the studio.

Maddy's heart was in her boots as she rushed towards the contestants' room. Don't let me bump into anyone who knows I shouldn't be here, she begged. She went into the contestants' room – so far so good – into the office, switched on the computer, took a quick look at the floppy disks in the box – one of them was labled ‹dBase files back up› –, called up dBase, put the disk into the disk drive, called up the file – what was the command again? She gave the ‹DISPLAY› command and built the search condition. Please let it be right, she prayed.

There it was: Andy Korbel. That definitely wasn't the same name as the one Manni had written down. She copied the details as fast as she could onto a piece of paper, quit dBase, took the disk out, switched off the computer and left the office. She couldn't believe she had managed it all so quickly.

Im Studio war die Stimmung gereizt. Manni und Henk waren wieder da, alles war bereit für die Aufnahme, nur Maddy fehlte. «Where the hell is she?», the floor manager shouted at Derek.

«Gone to the loo», Derek lied. He felt uneasy because he hadn't kept an eye on the contestants. «It's no use shouting at me, I can't exactly go with her, can I?»

«Well where was Joanne, then? Why do we have two contestant coordinators, for God's sake?»

«Joanne was looking after Henk with the bloody nose – remember?»

«Look, in future none of these kids is to leave the studio during an interruption in the recording. Got it?», the floor manager roared at Derek.

Warum dauerte es so lange bei ihr, dachte Manni. Er hatte Angst, dass sie gleich eine Suchmannschaft losschicken würden. Manni starrte auf die Tür. Da war Maddy. Sie strahlte übers ganze Gesicht. Manni und Henk atmeten erleichtert durch.

«Well I'm glad you're happy about it», grumbled Derek.

«Glad about what?», Maddy answered hesitantly. Surely he didn't know…

«About keeping us all waiting. Nearly cost me my job. You don't leave the studio in future until I say so, okay?»

«Jawohl!» She clicked her heels together and saluted smartly.

Der Rest der Aufnahme verlief ohne Komplikationen. Die Floppies waren wie ausgewechselt. Nichts mehr schien ihnen misslingen zu können. Ihre Kette wurde immer länger, während die Rockets leer ausgingen. Maddy, Manni und Henk waren im Halbfinale.

Sechstes Kapitel

****

in dem nicht viel passiert
but in which everybody gets into position

Florian and Sakina were waiting for Maddy in the Butler's house when she got home. She told them about the Floppies' victory and their discovery on the computer.

«So I was right after all», Sakina exclaimed, «there can be no doubt about it now. There are two Andys.»

Florian und Maddy nickten zustimmend.

«But it doesn't make sense, does it?», Maddy sighed, «why would anyone want to go to the trouble of exchanging one contestant for another?»

«Vielleicht ist er nur krank geworden», spekulierte Florian.

«But then they could have still shown him in the Qualifying Round and later said that they had to bring in a substitute for the quarterfinal, couldn't they?», Maddy argued.

Maddy ist voll darauf abgefahren, dachte Florian überrascht, und dabei hatte sie am Sonntag noch gemeint, dass Sakina spinnt. Klar, es gab zwei Andys, und man wollte ihnen und den Zuschauern weismachen, dass es den ersten nie gegeben hatte. Aber warum? Auch Florian fiel keine Antwort ein.

Maddy went to phone Una to tell her about the events of the day.

«Was meinst du, Sakina», überlegte Florian, «wir haben doch jetzt die Namen und Adressen von den beiden Andys, vielleicht sollten wir einfach mal sehen, was die so machen.»

«You mean we should observe them? But they know us.»

«Das stimmt natürlich. Aber keiner von denen hat bisher Henk, Maddy oder Manni gesehen.»

«That's true. Their Qualifying Round hasn't been shown on telly yet nor have they had to play against them.»

«Hmm.» Florian überlegte einen Augenblick. «Morgen zeichnen sie das Viertelfinale von den Jokers gegen den Fanclub auf, am Tag drauf ist das von den Argonauts gegen die Tigers, und dann kommen wir dran. Ich habe übrigens Joanne gefragt, warum das in dieser Reihenfolge passiert, und sie hat gesagt, dass das nur davon abhängt, wie sie die Kandidaten am billigsten nach London einfliegen können. Warum müssen ausgerechnet wir in unserem Viertelfinale auf die Cyclists treffen! Gegen die haben wir bestimmt keine Chance. Die hatten die längste Kette.»

«Just you wait and see», replied Sakina cooly, «but tomorrow...»

«Da sind weder wir noch Henk, Manni und Maddy im Studio», fiel ihr Florian ins Wort.

«Nor are the Argonauts», Sakina completed the train of thought, «so we could take a look at what the wrong Andy – Andy Hedley – is up to as well. Maybe he'll be meeting the real Andy – Andy Korbel – for tea, who knows?»

When Maddy came back from phoning Una, Sakina told her about the idea.

«That's fine with me if we follow them around for a while», she said and got up to go.

«Nicht sofort!», protestierte Florian.

«I'm not stupid, you know, I have to phone Henk, Manni and Una to tell them to come around here tomorrow after breakfast, haven't I?»

Am nächsten Morgen wurden sie sich schnell über ihr Vorgehen einig. Manni, Maddy und Henk sollten den ersten Andy beschatten, den sie noch nie gesehen hatten. Una, who had already arranged to go shopping with her aunt when Maddy got her on the phone would go along and stay with them long enough to identify Andy Korbel as soon as he came out of the house. Then she would have to leave. It was just as well, because. Andy Korbel, so they assumed, knew her from the Qualifying Round.

Florian und Sakina würden sich Andy Hedley, dem ‹falschen› Andy, an die Fersen heften. Sie mussten dabei besonders vorsichtig sein, denn er hatte bestimmt mehrmals das Video von ihrem Ausscheidungsspiel gesehen, sodass er wusste, gegen wen er da angeblich gespielt hatte.

Una didn't like the idea of Sakina hanging around with Florian all day, but there was little she could do about it. Manni rief außerdem Derek an und fragte, ob er am Tag darauf ins Studio kommen dürfe, um die technische Seite der Fernsehproduktion kennen zu lernen. Er wollte später schließlich einmal Aufnahmeleiter oder so werden, flunkerte er.

«Brilliant idea», Una congratulated him, «that way you can keep an eye on Andy Hedley in the studio tomorrow as well.»

Andy Hedley wohnte in der Nähe des Bahnhofs West Norwood. Von den Butlers aus hatten Florian und Sakina es nicht allzu weit. Maddy, Una, Manni and Henk had much further to travel. They had to cross half of London until they reached a small side street in the borough of Islington where Andy Korbel lived.

«It's difficult not to be noticed here», moaned Una when they were standing at the corner, no café, no amusement arcade, no nothing, just one house after the next. «Where are you supposed to hide?» But they were lucky. Una had just said that when a fellow, about the same height as Manni, thin with brown hair and listening to a walkman, walked out of the house. He slammed the door shut behind him.

«That's him», Una whispered loudly to the others.

«Great», said Maddy, «so you can go now. Enjoy the shopping.»

Florian und Sakina waren schon bei der zweiten Cola. Irgendwas mussten sie in dem kleinen Imbiss schräg gegenüber von dem Haus, in dem Andy Hedley angeblich wohnte, ja schließlich konsumieren. Blöde Warterei, dachte Florian.

Maddy wondered how they would be able to follow Andy Korbel in that area without been seen, but she didn't have to worry long. He walked straight to the next bus stop. Soon the number 4 bus to Waterloo pulled up. Andy got in and went upstairs. Manni, Henk und Maddy blieben unten. So sah er sie nicht, und sie waren trotzdem sicher, dass er nicht unbemerkt an ihnen vorbeikonnte.

Sakina and Florian were already sipping their third Coke when they saw a girl, about the same age as Sakina with shoulder length blond hair, ringing the bell on the door of Andy's house. «I wonder who that is», Sakina said, automatically lowering her voice.

«Bestimmt seine Freundin. Die hängen sich jetzt vor die Glotze und ziehen sich massenweise Videos rein, und wir sitzen hier und trinken Coke, bis wir braun werden», flüsterte er zurück.

«I don't suppose she can hear us at the other side of the road!», Sakina laughed with her normal voice. She thought that Florian was probably right, but even if they had to sit there for ages, she didn't mind. Hanging around with him wasn't bad. Maddy often gave out about him, calling him an arrogant, spoilt, rich kid, but whenever Sakina was with him she found him very nice.

Their thoughts about having to drink Coke for hours were wrong. A few minutes after the girl arrived, the door opened again. This time she left with Andy Hedley. Florian sprang auf und bezahlte die Colas. Sakina kept her eye on Andy and the girl. They walked towards the train station with their arms around one another.

«Nicht noch eine Verkehrsmarmelade», klagte Manni, als der Bus Nummer 4 langsam über die Waterloo Bridge kroch.

Maddy didn't understand what he was saying.

«Joke», Henk came to her assistance, «he means ‹traffic jam›.»

Maddy gave Manni her best and broadest Ginger Marley smile.

«Hoffentlich fährt der nicht zum Bahnhof Waterloo und dann per Zug weiter», sagte Manni schnell.

But Andy got out at the next stop on the bridge. The three shadowers got off, too. Henk marched straight after Andy but Manni and Maddy called him back.

«Nicht so offensichtlich», warnte Manni.

«He's not supposed to know we are after him», Maddy complained.

«Onzin», Henk muttered under his breath, «do you really think we are going to find out anything anyway? It probably doesn't make any difference at all whether we hide behind walls and trees or not.»

Andy lief direkt auf einen riesigen Betonklotz zu. O Gott, was ist denn das für eine Kaserne, dachte Manni.

«The National Theatre», said Maddy surprised, «why is he going in there?»

«Ins Theater?», wiederholte Manni erstaunt und überlegte, «vielleicht kennt er da jemand oder will Karten buchen oder weiß der Kuckuck.»

When she heard *Kuckuck*, Maddy started to make a flapping movement with her arms and run around in circles. Henk and Manni just stared at her for a second and then burst out laughing.

Andy had gone in the door of the building by now, so the three had to hurry after him. Concrete was everywhere. And glass. Lots of glass through which the trees by the Thames, the skateboarders and the seagulls could be seen.

Sobald er im Gebäude war, änderte Manni seine Meinung von der Kaserne. Der Betonklotz war voller Leben. Leute tranken Kaffee, eine Band spielte Jazz – Jazz im Theater und das zur Mittagszeit, dachte Manni –, und auf allen Ebenen schien es Cafés, Restaurants, Bars und Buchläden zu geben.

«You could easily get lost here», Henk remarked.

«Yes, you could», Maddy replied and then remembering that they wanted to speak German when they were hot on someone's trail, she added «und wir haben unseren Verdacht verloren.»

«Unseren Verdächtigen», lachte Manni, «nee, der läuft da gerade die Treppe hoch.» Sie liefen ihm nach.

Luckily Andy Hedley and his girlfriend went to the far end of the platform to wait for the train to Victoria. That meant that Florian and Sakina could hang around at the near end and not look too suspicious. Soon the train arrived and all four got in. Bei jedem Halt stieg Florian aus, um nachzusehen, ob die beiden den Zug verließen. Streatham Hill – Balham – Wandsworth Common: sie blieben drin.

‹Welcome to the busiest Station in Britain. Welcome to Clapham Junction› stand auf einem Schild, als sie in den nächsten Bahnhof einfuhren. Na, da könnte ja mal was passieren, dachte Florian, damit wir auch mal *busy* werden. Und tatsächlich stiegen die beiden aus und gingen durch die Unterführung zum Gleis 10.

«That's the platform for Waterloo», said Sakina, «maybe they are culture vultures and want to go to one of the theatres or concert halls there.»

«Auch das noch», stöhnte Florian. Was immer Kultur-*vultures* waren, ins Theater wollte er ihnen bestimmt nicht folgen.

Sie hielten Abstand und hätten dadurch fast den Zug verpasst, der gerade einfuhr.

Andy Korbel continued to climb the stairs. On the next landing was a small bookshop and a bar. Andy walked straight over to the bar. He knows his way round here, thought Maddy. The three of them ‹looked› at books while keeping an eye on Andy. He bought something to drink and walked to a door which led outside.

Er ging auf eine Terrasse mit wunderschönem Blick auf die Themse und setzte sich auf die letzte der vielen Holzbänke, die noch frei waren. Bänke wie im Biergarten, dachte Manni – und das im Betondschungel. Was sollten sie jetzt machen – keine

Bank mehr frei, aber nur so rumstehen konnten sie ja auch nicht.

«Look, there is another terrace up there. We should still be able to see him from it», Maddy whispered to Manni, forgetting that the three of them were supposed to speak German. Der nickte.

Von der Bayliss Terrace oben hatten sie einen guten Blick auf die Olivier Terrace, auf der Andy saß. Er saß da, trank aus seinem Glas und hörte Walkman.

Maddy looked around. They were alone on the terrace.

«Maybe this is it», said Henk.

«This is what?», Maddy asked.

«It. Maybe he's just come here to have a drink, admire the view and then he'll go home.»

Manni warf ihm einen skeptischen Blick zu. «Das glaube ich nicht. Wer würde eine Busreise unternehmen, bloß um irgendwo allein rumzusitzen und dann wieder nach Hause zu fahren?»

Henk shrugged his shoulders and pushed his glasses up onto the bridge of his nose. He didn't say anything. Does he do that, wondered Maddy. Go off by himself a lot? She realized that she knew very little about him.

Suddenly there was real action on the terrace below. A man, carrying a cup of coffee, walked over to Andy's table. He put his hand on the boy's shoulder.

«Achtung», zischte Manni, «der Kontakt ist da.» Was das für ein Kontakt sein sollte, wusste er allerdings nicht.

Andy looked up und then slowly, almost reluctantly, turned off the walkman. The similarity between Andy and the man was unmistakable. It could only be his father, Maddy decided. The man kept his hand on Andy's shoulder for a while before he sat down. He now had his back to the three shadowers. They could see Andy's face, which didn't look too happy. For a while neither the boy nor the man seemed to say anything. The man drank some coffee. Then he started talking to Andy. Andy shook his head. The man continued talking – asking something, perhaps.

So ein Mist, dachte Manni, von hier aus versteht man kein Wort. Andy schüttelte weiterhin dauernd mit dem Kopf und stand auf. Wollte er weggehen? Der Mann legte seine Hand auf Andys Arm. Bleib doch, schien das zu bedeuten. Andy setzte sich wieder. Eine Zeit lang schien keiner der beiden etwas zu sagen.

«Hat einer von euch 'ne Idee, worüber die reden?», fragte Manni. Maddy and Henk shook their heads and kept looking at the terrace below.

Nichts tat sich. Manni sah zur Themse hinüber. Ein toller Ausblick. Und viele interessant aussehende Gebäude am anderen Ufer. Er kannte keines davon. Gut, dass das kein Schultrip ist, dachte Manni, Herr Münchberg hätte sicher sofort den Führer in der Hand und würde Entstehungsgeschichte, Daten, Architekten und alles vorlesen. Gut, dass er nicht da war.

«Hey», Maddy gave Manni a nudge, «it looks as if they might be throwing a party now.» Another man who was about the same age as Andy's ‹father› had walked over to the table where Andy and his ‹father› were sitting. Andy's ‹father› stood up to greet him.

«Wer ist das?», fragte Manni. «Von hier aus kriegen wir nichts raus. Man hört ja nichts. Wir müssen näher ran.»

They decided that Manni and Maddy should go down to the terrace below to see if they could hear any of the conversation. They could pretend to be a couple just admiring the view. Manni könnte sich in der Nähe des Tisches ans Geländer stellen und Maddy könnte mit ihrer Kamera ein Foto von ihm machen. Im Hintergrund würde man dann nicht nur die Themse, sondern auch Andy, seinen Vater – oder wer immer das auch war – und den anderen Mann haben. Und so könnten sie vielleicht auch einen Teil der Unterhaltung aufschnappen. Henk blieb auf der Bayliss Terrace, um alles von oben im Auge zu behalten.

«And if they get up and go, what then?», Henk asked.

The three friends wanted to find out exactly who the men were and to see if they could get any further information by following them, so they arranged that Manni would shadow the second man, Maddy would take the ‹father› and Henk would stay on Andy's tracks.

With their arms around one another, Maddy and Manni strolled around the Olivier Terrace. I could get used to this, thought Maddy as she snuggled into Manni. They did a whole round first, so as not to look suspicious. When they walked past Andy's table they heard the second man saying in a pleading tone: «You've got to understand what we are saying to you. You have to trust us.»

Andy responded with a sarcastic noise.

Manni versuchte so langsam wie möglich mit seiner neuen Freundin an dem Tisch vorbeizuziehen, aber auch die langsamste Schnecke ist mal am Ziel. Sie gerieten außer Hörweite.

Bei der zweiten Runde wollten sie den Trick mit dem Foto versuchen. Manni ging am Tisch vorbei und rief: «Is here okay, love?» Von dort, wo er jetzt stand, konnte er alles gut verstehen.

«Perfect, darling.» Maddy giggled to herself. While she

fiddled round with the camera her ears were wide open for what was being said.

«If you would stop going on about trust and tell me something real», hörten sie Andy sagen. Er war ganz rot im Gesicht und wirkte wütend.

«Der ‹Vater› antwortete ruhig: «Andy, if I could tell you more I would, but I can't.»

«It's not enough», gab Andy aufgeregt zurück.

«It will have to be», das war der zweite Mann.

«Smile!», Maddy shouted to Manni. She took a picture.

«Look, this isn't getting us anywhere», redete der ‹Vater› auf Andy ein, «what's done is done and you just have to accept it.»

«We'll see about that.» Immer noch klang Andy trotzig und aufgeregt.

«What do you mean?», hakte der zweite Mann nach.

«You'll see.»

«Stay where you are, I'll take another one», Maddy called to Manni.

«Look, Andy, I've told you…»

«You've told me nothing», unterbrach der ihn, «nothing except that I have to trust you and believe you. Well, we'll see about that.»

Die Blicke von Andys ‹Vater› und dem zweiten Mann trafen sich. Beide sahen besorgt aus.

«Look», fing der ‹Vater› wieder an, «we don't want to make a scene. Let's continue our discussion tonight. Hmm? I'll be home at, let me see now… it will be some time after half past ten, okay?»

Maddy had taken three or four pictures already. Should she boss Manni into letting her take even more? She took a quick look at Andy. He was sitting there, saying nothing. His ‹father› took out his wallet and gave him a couple of notes.

«Look, son, why don't you go and buy yourself some records now and we'll talk about all this later?»

Home. Son. Das ist eindeutig, kombinierte Manni. Das ist Andys Vater.

Andy took the money without even looking at it, stood up and, without saying another word to the men, walked off.

Ganz plötzlich waren auch Maddy und Manni mit ihrer Fotografiererei fertig. So schnell, wie das für ein verliebtes Paar gerade noch möglich ist, bummelten sie um die nächste Ecke und rannten dann auf die Bayliss Terrace hinauf. Henk war schon weg, offenbar hinter Andy her. Auf der unteren Terrasse verabschiedeten sich gerade die beiden Männer.

«It's time for us to say goodbye, darling», said Maddy in a choked voice and wiped an imaginary tear from her cheek. She went to follow the man they now knew was Andy's father.

Chapter seven

****

*in which Maddy has to cross a bridge
und in dem Florian der Spaß an seinem Berliner vergeht*

Im Bahnhof Waterloo herrschte ein ziemliches Gedränge, und Florian und Sakina mussten sich ganz schön anstrengen, um Andy Hedley und das blonde Mädchen nicht aus den Augen zu verlieren. Im Augenblick standen sie in der Schlange am Croissant-Kiosk.

«Come on, I'll buy you a doughnut», said Sakina and pointed to the Quicksnack counter where the queue was much shorter, «after all, you are a doughnut yourself, aren't you?»

«Hä?»

«Well, you are a ‹Berliner› which is a kind of doughnut, isn't it?» – «Ha ha. Woher kennst du denn ein Wort wie ‹Berliner›?», fragte Florian.

«You won't believe this, but I learnt it in a grammar class. Our German teacher was trying to teach us the difference between using ‹ein› and using no article at all, and he said that if you want to say ‹I am a Berliner› you have to say ‹Ich bin Berliner›, because if you say ‹Ich bin ein Berliner› it means ‹I am a doughnut›. And that's what the American president said when he visited Berlin soon after the wall had been built.»

«Hm», brummte Florian. Darüber hatte er noch nie nachgedacht. Aber so ganz konnte das ja nicht stimmen; schließlich hatte jeder verstanden, was Präsident Kennedy gemeint hatte.

Andy und seine Freundin hatten endlich ihre Croissants gekauft und marschierten in Richtung Ausgang. Florian und Sakina hinterher.

Maddy followed Andy Korbel's father along the Riverside Walk, keeping her distance. He arrived at the long tubelike covered jetty to the Festival Pier, which was the station for the river bus on the south bank. He disappeared into it. Maddy saw the river bus approaching on the Thames. She saw the man sprint and jump onto the boat. Shit! She wouldn't make it. What now? The boat sounded its horn twice and pulled out. She knew that it would stop again on the other side of the river at the Charing Cross Pier station. She looked around. There was always the Hungerford Bridge which trains and pedestrians used to cross the river. If she raced across it… A shiver ran down her spine. Her, Maddy, race across the Hungerford Bridge? But it had to be done. She had said she would shadow that man, and shadow him she would.

Manni folgte dem zweiten Mann durch den Betondschungel. Überall gab es Wendeltreppen, die irgendwohin führten, Hinweisschilder noch und noch, Wege, die sich kreuzten. Der Mann und Manni folgten den Schildern ‹Queen Elizabeth Hall› und ‹Royal Festival Hall›. Sie kamen zu einem noch größeren Betonmonster, auf dessen unterster Ebene sie sich befanden.

Maddy ran along the Riverside Walk until she came to the steps of the bridge. A red, normal-looking bridge. Up to the two flights of stairs, two at a time, past the white signpost at the top which read PEDESTRIANS ONLY, CYCLING, SKATEBOARDING, ROLLER SKATING PROHIBITED. The first couple of yards over the bridge were okay. Under it you could still see the Riverside Walk. But then she saw the water coming up ahead. Oh God, why was I the one chosen to follow him, she asked herself. She hated bridges and she hated heights. The pedestrian part wasn't more than about one and a half metres wide. She ran along the bridge wondering how secure the red railings at the edge were which came up to her shoulder. The wind blew sheets of newspaper against them. Looking down to the right now she could see the brown water. A Coca-Cola can bounced on the tide. The water had a dark and threatening look.

Florian und Sakina folgten dem Pärchen durch den Hauptausgang und durch eine Passage, in der es herrlich nach frisch geröstetem Kaffee roch, was Florian dazu führte, ein großes Stück von seinem Doughnut abzubeißen. Weiter ging es um die Ecke, eine Treppe hinunter und durch eine weitere dunkle Passage. Sakina stole a sidewards glance at Florian. How would he react to what was coming next, she wondered.

Als sie aus der Passage auf einen runden Platz traten, kam Florian der Doughnut wieder hoch. Es stank stark und eindeutig nach Urin, auf roten Bänken um den Platz herum saßen und lagen Männer und Frauen, völlig zerlumpt, verschmutzt, vor ihnen jede Menge Bierdosen, um sie herum viele Hunde, die besser ernährt zu sein schienen als ihre Besitzer.

«Could you spare some change please, sir», bettelte einer der Zerlumpten höflich einen Mann im blauen Anzug an. Der sah durch ihn durch, als wäre er Luft, und ging schnell weiter. Florian war unwillkürlich stehen geblieben. Er schluckte mehrmals. «This is the ugly side of modern Britain», said Sakina, «but don't stop», she urged him on, «we have to keep moving.» Wie in Trance ging Florian hinter ihr her.

The blue and white river bus was crossing the Thames, heading towards Charing Cross Pier station. Would Maddy make it in time? Don't look down, she kept saying to herself as she raced across the bridge, don't look down, but her eyes were drawn constantly to the driftwood and litter being swept along by the water. She knew if she looked straight ahead she would be alright, but the water was like a magnet to her eyes even if it made her feel sick to look at it. A cool wind was blowing but she was covered in sweat. Her legs felt weak and she was dizzy. She knew she had to keep going no matter how sick she felt. It will all be over when I get to the other side, she consoled herself. But the other side didn't seem to be getting any closer although she was running as fast as she could.

Mannis Mann ging zielstrebig auf eine eiserne Tür zu und verschwand hinter ihr. Kein Schild gab an, wohin sie führte. Manni überlegte einen Augenblick. Sicher ein Hintereingang zu einem dieser Kulturtempel, dachte er. Was hatte er zu verlieren? Nichts. Er lief hinüber, öffnete langsam die Tür, spähte in den Raum, konnte nichts erkennen, hörte nichts. Er überlegte einen Moment, sah sich um, um sicher zu sein, dass ihn keiner beobachtete, und ging hinein. Leise zog er die Tür hinter sich zu. Es wurde sehr dunkel.

The river bus was only slightly ahead of Maddy. Would she be able to catch up with it? All of a sudden a distant rumbling noise could be heard getting louder and louder. The bridge startet to vibrate. The rumbling noise burst into an ear-shattering boom. The entire bridge shook as a train came thundering through on the tracks to Maddy's left. She stepped instinctively to the right and knocked against the railings. She looked down.

The water was still rushing below. Maddy surpressed a scream. KTHUMP KTHUMP. The noise of the train was deafening. Just keep running, she said to herself. Don't look down, don't mind the train. She was terrified. All this time, people were crossing the bridge in both directions, as if it was the most normal footpath in the world. Kids rushed past her on skateboards. She kept running.

Florian und Sakina überquerten den Platz und gingen eine Rampe hinauf, die zum Südufer der Themse mit seinen Theatern, Konzertsälen und Kinos führte. Der Gestank nahm zu. Links und rechts von der Rampe lagen große Pappkartons, zusammengestellt, als wären sie eine kleine Siedlung. An einigen Stellen lugten unter Haufen von schmutzigen Decken Köpfe oder Füße hervor. «Give us some spare change, please», hörte Florian ein junges Mädchen zu einem der Passanten sagen. Der beachtete sie nicht.

Florian schnürte es die Kehle zu.

Sakina took his arm. «Cardboard city», she said, «it's bad enough now in the summer, but you can imagine what it's like when the weather gets cold. We passed by here one December night last year. There were all these barrels with fires in them and groups of people standing around them to try to get warm. Awful.»

Florian ging jetzt schneller. Sie durften Andy Hedley nicht aus den Augen verlieren. Sie kamen ans Ende der Rampe. Ein großer Wegweiser zeigte das große Angebot an Kultur: National Theatre, Royal Festival Hall, Museum of the Moving Image, National Film Theatre, Queen Elizabeth Hall. Florian warf den Rest des Doughnuts in einen Papierkorb. «Come on», Sakina pulled him along, «we mustn't lose sight of them.»

Andy and his girlfriend had just joined a queue. Florian warf einen Blick zurück. Der letzte Bissen kam ihm hoch.

The river bus had arrived at Charing Cross Pier boat station. Maddy ran straight into a middle-aged man carrying a briefcase as she rushed towards the stairs at the end of the bridge. «Sorry», she muttered. She raced across the road and just missed being run over by a Range Rover. At the station she shouted to the man at the ticket office in a breathless voice that she would pay at the other end. She ran up the stairs and jumped onto the moving pier just in time to see the river bus drive away from the pier. She could see Andy's father sitting in the back of the boat. «Shit», she said as she dropped down onto the floor, totally exhausted and feeling weak after her ordeal.

Sakina and Florian waited for a while until a few other people had joined the queue and then took their place. «Wofür steht man denn hier an?», fragte Florian leise. «The Museum of the Moving Image», Sakina answered. She was looking forward to this part of the shadowing exercise.

«*Museum*? Uuagh. Ich hasse Museen.» Sakina smiled. «This isn't a normal museum. It's all about making films and TV. It's fantastic – I've been here twice already. You'll enjoy it.»

Florian sah sie skeptisch an. «Aber es heißt Museum – und alle Museen sind langweilig.»

«You'll see. But you have to be careful before you say anything, when we are in there. You'd never know who's just around the corner, whether someone is behind you or whether you are appearing on a screen.»

Appearing on a screen? Wie gut, dass ich wieder meinen telegenen Pullover anhabe, dachte Florian.

By the time Maddy caught her breath again, she was very disappointed. Back to base, I suppose, she said to herself. Maybe the others had better luck. On the way home she took the film out of the camera and brought it to her local One Hour Film developer.

Mannis Augen gewöhnten sich schnell an das Halbdunkel. Eine Wendeltreppe ging nach oben; von dort führte ein Gang in einen Raum, der voll mit den verschiedensten Sachen stand. Er stolperte über etwas, was sich beim genaueren Hinsehen als eine weiße Pappwolke entpuppte. Er hörte Schritte. Schnell versteckte er sich hinter einem Vorhang.

«God only knows what he sees in her», hörte er einen der beiden Männer sagen, die eine große Kiste hineinschleppten, «just another bimbo he's picked up somewhere, I suppose.»

«She's only done kiddies' stuff on TV so far», antwortete der andere, «and before you know it, she's on the stage of the Queen Elizabeth Hall.»

«Mind you», fuhr der erste fort, während sie die Kiste absetzten, «it's bloody 'orrible stuff anyway, a real matinee for geriatrics.»

Sie verließen den Abstellraum. Manni atmete tief durch. Hinter dem Vorhang waren lauter Abendkleider gewesen, die alle sehr stark nach einer Mischung aus Schminke, Schweiß und Mottenkugeln rochen. Vorsichtig, um nichts umzuwerfen, ging er den beiden Männern nach. Eine Tür stand halb offen, von dort kamen Stimmen. Manni spähte vorsichtig in den Raum – er sah in einen großen Zuschauerraum, der dunkel war. Auf der Bühne standen ein Klavier und ein Schlagzeug, Techniker waren damit beschäftigt, Mikrofone zu installieren, jemand probierte gerade die Scheinwerfer aus. Aber wo war der Mann, hinter dem er her war? Manni sah ihn nicht und wollte sich auch nicht zu weit hinter der Tür hervorwagen. Da probte einer der Beleuchter einen Scheinwerferschwenk ins Publikum – der Mann saß in der ersten Reihe und unterhielt sich, Manni stockte der Atem, mit Ginger Marley.

Achtes Kapitel

****

in dem Florian vergisst, dass Museen langweilig sind,
and in which Sakina does something really daring

Florian took out his wallet at the ticket office and paid £ 2.50 each for himself and Sakina. When she tried to give him the money, he refused to take it.

«Wenn ihr immer meint, dass ich ein *rich kid* bin, dann sollt ihr wenigstens was davon haben», sagte er. Sakina blushed. «I never called you that.»

«Wow!», staunte Florian, als sie im ersten Raum eine Treppe hinuntergingen und auf einem Fußboden landeten, der ganz aus schwarzen und weißen Quadraten bestand. Zur Mitte hin wurden sie immer kleiner und liefen schließlich zusammen, um einen Pfeil zu formen, der auf ein riesiges Auge auf der anderen Seite des Raumes deutete. Wie hypnotisiert ging er auf das Auge zu. Es war so gebaut, dass man in die Pupille hinein-schauen konnte: Ihre Wände bestanden aus Spiegeln und ganz hinten war ein Fernsehbildschirm angebracht. Es war, als blickte man in einen tiefen Spiegel-Tunnel, in dem die Bilder tausendmal von einer Wand zur anderen flitzten.

Sakina looked around. Andy Hedley and his girlfriend were engrossed in some shadow puppets in the far corner. «Look up, Florian», she said. Er schaute nach oben. Dort liefen schwarze und weiße Strahlen von einem Zentrum auseinander und wur-den dabei immer breiter.

«Keep looking up and move around», Sakina ordered.

Florian probierte es. Während er sich bewegte, veränderte sich das Muster. Ihm wurde ganz schwindelig. All of a sudden Sakina took his arm firmly and propelled him into a dark corner where spooky music was playing for a magic lantern show.

«For goodness sake», she whispered to Florian, «they nearly bumped into us. We'll have to be more careful. They shouldn't see us before we want them to.»

Florian nickte etwas benommen. Die Muster jagten noch durch seinen Kopf.

The bus in which Andy Korbel and Henk were travelling took ages to get Piccadilly Circus. There Andy got out. So did Henk. Andy manœuvred his way through the cars and people to a shop called ‹Tower Records›. It was difficult, but Henk managed to follow him. Through glass doors, up some steps then wow! Henk had never seen anything like it before! He had entered what seemed to him to be the largest record shop in the world. While music was blaring out of loudspeakers in every corner, hundreds of neon rainbows flashed non-stop at him, trying to divert his attention away from the multi-screens which were displaying all the latest videos. Henk was stuck to the spot, feeling the rhythm of the music beating up from the floor through his body and looking from one screen to another. Andy bought two CDs and then went up the stairs to the jazz section. Cool white lights, low ceiling, a slow blues number was playing to the handful of quiet customers. I'd love to have a look at the classical section, thought Henk, but he had to keep an eye on Andy who didn't need much time to find what he was looking for. He paid for three more CDs and left. Andy did no more shopping. He went straight home to Islington. Henk followed him all the way but decided that there was nothing more he could do. If he had just bought the pile of records which Andy had, he wouldn't leave the house again for days. He started the long journey back to Maddy's.

«Come on, Florian», Sakina hissed for the umpteenth time. Honestly, for someone who said he didn't like museums, he was getting more than stuck at several points in this one. «We do have a job to do here, you know», she added.

«Sorry.» Florian fühlte sich ertappt. Sie waren dem ‹falschen› Andy nun schon durch einige Räume gefolgt, die die Anfänge des Kinos zeigten, und Florian musste zugeben, dass *dieses* Museum viel interessanter als andere Museen und sogar interessanter als die Beschattung von Andy war.

Durch den Raum mit den frühen Hollywood Stars, die Florian alle nicht kannte, waren sie den beiden zu einer Ausstellungsfläche zum Thema Film und der Erste Weltkrieg gefolgt. Dort hatten sie eine Frontszene nachgestellt und durch periskopartige Öffnungen sah man verschiedene Filme, die während des Krieges über den Krieg gedreht worden waren. Mit lauter bösen Deutschen. Sakina felt very awkward in the First World War room with Florian. There was all kinds of material about the evil Germans and films were showing about events like the sinking of the Lusitania. She didn't know what to say.

There was nobody there when Maddy arrived home. She tried to go on reading her *Knowledge from A–Z* but she couldn't get excited about whether it was the Volga or the Danube which was the longest river in Europe. She switched on the telly but all that was on was a programme about wildlife, a chat show, horse-racing and a children's show. She wasn't in the mood for any of it. She tried to phone Una but only got her aunt's answering machine. She paced the living-room restlessly. How were the others getting on?

«Roll up, roll up comrades», rief eine Stimme mit russischem Akzent. Eine Frau in einem langen grauen Rock und grauem Pullover, mit rotem Kopftuch und Nickelbrille lief direkt auf Florian zu. «Comrade, come into our train and see the good work that our government is doing for the people. You will see the wonderful improvements for the workers. You are probably a farm worker yourself, am I right?» Florian schaute sie verdutzt an und sagte nichts. «Well», fuhr sie fort, «come and see our film about the amazing new cream machine.»

Sakina grabbed Florian by the arm and dragged him into the railway carriage. «Come on», she whispered, «the two of them have come in here, too.»

Florian saß auf einer der Holzbänke in dem dunklen Eisenbahnabteil und wusste nicht mehr, was los war. War die Frau eben eine Museumswärterin oder was? Es lief gerade ein Stummfilm, in dem tatsächlich eine Maschine die Hauptrolle spielte. Man sah die freudeüberströmten Gesichter der Bauern im Film, als die sahen, wie die Sahne von der Milch getrennt wurde. Während der Film lief, hörte Florian die Frau mit dem russischen Akzent immer wieder auf die Leute einreden. Verrückt! Zwei Gestalten standen vorne und verließen das Eisenbahnabteil. Andy und seine Freundin, so glaubte Florian im Flimmerlicht zu erkennen. Er stand sofort auf. Sakina pulled him down saying: «Not so fast. Wait a minute, for goodness sake.»

Sie folgten den beiden zur großen Eingangshalle eines Kinos aus den dreißiger Jahren, in der es wenig Versteckmöglichkeiten gab. Florian und Sakina warteten deshalb draußen, machten aber ab und zu die Tür auf, um zu sehen, ob Andy und seine Freundin schon weggegangen waren. Jedes Mal, wenn sie sie sahen, machten sie die Tür schnell wieder zu und warteten noch ein bisschen.

«You know what you look like?», a voice asked. Florian and Sakina turned to see an old man in an old-fashioned suit. «Actors in a detective movie pretending they are shadowing someone.»

Sakina's jaw dropped open. Had they been that obvious? The old man continued:

«And a B-movie at that. Why are you following that young man and his giggly blonde girlfriend?»

Florian atmete tief durch. Gehörte dieser Mann mit dem altertümlichen Anzug zum Museum, sollte er als eine Art Platzanweiser des alten Kinos die Leute anmachen? Oder war das auch ein Besucher? Oder beobachtete noch jemand anders Andy Hedley und damit zwangsläufig auch ihn und Sakina? In diesem Museum wusste man wirklich nicht, was echt und was gespielt war.

Florian fiel so schnell keine Antwort ein, and Sakina didn't say anything either. «I know, I should mind my own business», the old man said as he walked away. «I shouldn't have asked in the first place.»

They waited for quite a while before they opened the door again. When they did, they saw that the two had left the room. They followed the arrows and found themselves inside a real cinema, dark and with several rows of red seats. They sat down. After all that walking and standing around, Sakina was glad that they could sit down for a moment. For a moment? It is well known that cinemas not only have the function of showing films. They often serve another purpose, too. Looking at Andy and his girlfriend, Sakina could see that they were using this cinema for its other purpose. They sat in the back row, kissing in the darkness. Sakina looked away. Florian schaute sich nach dem Pärchen um und sah, wie sie schmusten. Er drehte sich wieder um. Er und Sakina saßen in der Dunkelheit nebeneinander. Einfach nur so.

The doorbell rang. Maddy raced to open the door. It was her mother. «Thank goodness you are home, love», she said, «I left my keys in the office.»

Maddy must have looked disappointed, because her mother asked: «Where you expecting someone else?»

«Not really», Maddy answered, «Florian, maybe or Manni.»

«Have you been learning hard for the semifinal?»

Maddy nodded.

«Take it easy, love. Remember it is only a game», said her mother. Maddy went back into the living-room and started to read: ‹The First World War lasted from 1914 until 1918, the Second...› She yawned.

«Hey, look at that!», Sakina exclaimed. Florian sah nur einen leeren Ausstellungskasten. Darin stand eine unbekleidete Schaufensterpuppe. Na und? Sakina read aloud the notice pinned to the model: «Coming soon, the Wedding Dress worn by Kylie Minogue who played Charlene in ‹Neighbours›.» She sighed. «Do you get ‹Neighbours› in Germany?»

«Leider ja», brummte Florian. – «Don't you like it?»

Florian warf ihr einen skeptischen Blick zu. «Sag bloß nicht, dass du ‹Neighbours›-süchtig bist.» Sakina blushed and walked on.

Andy was standing over at the far side of the room explaining to his girlfriend how the television cameras worked. Of course, thought Sakina, that's why he brought her here. He wanted to show off about having been on television. Florian sah fasziniert zu, wie ein Mädchen über die Themse flog – genau wie Superman. Das Mädchen lag auf einer einfachen blauen Rampe und zappelte herum – und genau das sah man auf einem der Bildschirme. Auf einem zweiten sah man die Themse und auf einem dritten Bildschirm waren die beiden Bilder vereint: Das Mädchen flog die Themse entlang, über die Tower Bridge, über Boote, in Richtung Big Ben. Toll sah das aus.

«O ja, das mache ich auch», rief Florian und lief in Richtung Rampe, «Superman wollte ich schon immer mal spielen.»

«Are you crazy?», Sakina hissed holding him back, «remember what we said about being seen too early?»

Florian nickte. Sie hatte ja Recht. Leider. Er sah sich um. Ein Junge saß in einem Studio und wartete auf Fragen über neue Filme. Die Fragen waren schon vorher aufgenommen worden. Etwas später lief auf den Bildschirmen das Interview, und es sah so aus, als ob der Junge und der Interviewer zusammen aufgenommen worden waren. Hinten in der Ecke hing ein großes Schild. ‹SHOW YOUR OWN HOME VIDEO›, es sah dort aus wie in einem normalen Wohnzimmer. Und neben ihm wurde ein Mädchen von einer Kamera aufgenommen, die *stop-action camera* hieß. Kurz darauf sah man sie auf dem Bildschirm; ihre Bewegungen wirkten ruckartig, so als ob der Film zerschnitten worden wäre.

Sakina wondered what they should do. Should they just simply follow Andy? What would come out of it? She had an idea. She nudged Florian who seemed to be fascinated by the jerky movements of the stop-action camera, and pointed at Andy.

Andy und seine Freundin standen gerade vor einem kleinen Studio, in dem man sein Glück als Nachrichtensprecher versuchen konnte. Man setzte sich auf einen Stuhl neben ein Gerät, das aussah wie ein Overheadprojektor. Dieses Gerät warf Text auf eine Art Spiegel direkt vor der Kamera. Während man ihn vorlas, sah es so aus, als ob man direkt in die Kamera schaute und ganz frei sprach. Etwas später konnte man sich dann selbst draußen auf einem Bildschirm als perfekter Nachrichtensprecher bewundern. Andy sagte etwas zu seiner Freundin, was Florian und Sakina nicht mitbekommen konnten, und ging in das Studio.

I have to do it, Sakina said to herself, even though it is silly. It's more like the kind of stupid thing Una would do. She took a deep breath. Yes, she would do it. «This is our big moment», she whispered to Florian, «just wait till he comes out again.»

Florian und Sakina näherten sich langsam dem kleinen Studio. As soon as Sakina saw Andy's face on the screen she said in a loud voice: «That's Andy, that can only be Andy! He must be here somewhere!» Die Freundin schaute sie misstrauisch an. «Andy! I knew it was you – even without the make-up. What a coincidence!» Sakina walked over to him and gave him a big kiss.

Andy sah in diesem Moment nicht mehr aus wie der coole Fernsehstar von eben. «Oh hello», sagte er schwach. Sakina pretended to be insulted. «You haven't forgotten me – Sakina, remember. Florian is here, too.»

Florian trat einen Schritt vor. «Hallo, Andy», sagte er. «Of course I haven't forgotten», Andy said. Mann, hat der das aber schnell gecheckt, lobte ihn Florian. «I'd like to introduce my girlfriend Gillian.» Er wandte sich an das blonde Mädchen. «Gillian, this is Sakina and Florian. From the quiz, remember? You saw them on the telly on Sunday.»

Langsam nahm das Misstrauen auf dem Gesicht des Mädchens ab. «Oh yeah. Hi», sagte sie.

Sakina moved very close to Andy. «You never mentioned any girlfriend to me», she said in a hurt voice, «is that why you didn't phone?»

Florian war ganz baff. Die macht das unheimlich gut. So was hätte er eher Una zugetraut. Der arme Andy! Er stand einfach da und wusste nicht mehr, was er sagen sollte.

«Oh well», Sakina smiled sweetly at him, «maybe we can talk about it again sometime in the studio – you never know, we might meet again in the final. We won the Consolation Match, you know. Or you could give me that call you promised. You still have my number?»

Andy paused for only a second. «Of course I have, Sakina», he said. «Goodbye.» Er ging mit seiner unglücklich aussehenden Freundin weg.

«He's going to have a lot of explaining to do», laughed Sakina.

Chapter nine

****

in which similarity is a clue
und in dem Manni nicht weiß, was ein bimbo *ist*

After a while Henk arrived at Maddy's home. They compared notes and agreed that their shadowing hadn't been very successful. They then went to collect the photos and waited for the others to return.

Florian und Sakina kamen eine Stunde später. Beide waren sehr gut drauf und fielen einander mehrfach ins Wort, als sie ihre MOMI-Geschichte erzählten.

«Mann, der hat so belämmert aus der Wäsche geschaut, als Sakina ihn angemacht hat, der wusste echt nicht mehr, was Sache war. Er musste irgendwie mitspielen, weil er ja schlecht sagen konnte, dass er bei den Aufnahmen nicht dabei war.»

Maddy didn't really understand all that Florian had said but before she could ask, Sakina had interrupted him: «But at the same time he knew that I knew that he wasn't the real Andy. If I had fancied an Andy in the studio when that match was recorded, then it would have been Andy Korbel and not him. You should have seen his face! It was great. He knew that we hadn't met in the studio. But we were all pretending that we had. And his girlfriend was totally suspicious!»

Maddy looked at her friend in amazement. How daring Sakina had been! Not at all like her usual, quiet self. «Ich bin ja echt gespannt, was der jetzt macht», sagte Florian und dann: «Wo ist Manni? Und wie ist es eigentlich bei euch gelaufen?»

Henk and Maddy gave a brief report and showed them the photos.

«I think that after today's events the wrong Andy, Andy Hedley, will contact the people who organized the swop. He'll probably want to tell them that they have been found out», said Henk. «Sakina has really set the cat among the pigeons.»

Katze zwischen Tauben ist gut, dachte Florian. Woher hat der bloß solche Ausdrücke? «Gut, dass Manni morgen als Technikfan ins Studio geht», sagte er, «bei dem Viertelfinale mit dem falschen Andy tut sich bestimmt was. Wo zum Teufel steckt Manni bloß?»

Es klingelte. «Wie aufs Stichwort», kommentierte Florian while Maddy went to the door. It was Una who had just come back from the shopping spree with her aunt. They told her in detail what had happened. After they were finished there was still no sign of Manni. They started to worry. What had happened to him? Es wird ihm schon nichts passiert sein, beruhigte sich Florian, Manni kann auf sich aufpassen. Wahrscheinlich hing er irgendwo draußen vor einem Büro rum, in das der Mann reingegangen war, und wartete darauf, dass er wieder rauskam. Aber anrufen hätte er eigentlich mal können.

Mrs Butler stuck her head around the door. «All working hard preparing for the quiz?», she smiled. «They should try that method to get you to do your homework, it would be very effective.» «Yes Mum», Maddy said, «do you know what the capital of Romania is?»

Mrs Butler shrugged her shoulders and, as she closed the door, said «that's a question for Europeans, not for us British. By the way, have you lost the other German?»

For Europeans, dachte Florian, so'n Quatsch, die Engländer sind doch auch Europäer!

«Maddy», Henk asked when Mrs Butler had shut the door, «do you know your way around the local libraries?» Maddy shook her head.

«But I do», Sakina stepped in.

«Could we visit one or two of them tomorrow, do you think?», he asked her.

«Hast du 'ne Idee?», fragte Florian und fing sich einen protestierenden Blick von Una ein.

«Just a hunch», Henk replied. Florian wollte gerade fragen, was ein *hunch* war, als es klingelte.

Maddy raced to the door. Manni at last. At last? It was only a couple of hours ago since they had been walking around the South Bank as a ‹couple›. It seemed like weeks.

«Ihr werdet es nicht für möglich halten», stieß Manni hervor, «aber der zweite Mann kennt Ginger Marley!» Una wondered for a moment whether she could complain about Manni speaking German, but she thought he was probably too excited to say anything in English now anyway, so she would get Maddy to translate it for her afterwards.

Manni erzählte jetzt chronologisch. Er war gerade an der Stelle angekommen, wo er Ginger und den Mann entdeckt hatte. «Erst wollte ich sofort zurück. Aber dann dachte ich – vielleicht passiert ja noch mehr. Außerdem fing der Zuschauerraum an, sich zu füllen. Ich hab mich an der Bühne vorbei in den Zuschauerraum geschlichen, erst rumgehangen und mich dann auf einen freien Platz gesetzt.»

«Good to know», Maddy butted in, «if we ever want to go to a concert for free…»

«Aber bestimmt nicht zu so einem. Das war echt 'ne Strafe. ‹Festival of Popular Melodies› hieß das Konzert und die Zuschauer waren alle zwischen fünfundsiebzig und scheintot.

Und die Musik! Der Typ am Kontrabass, weiße Haare, sah aus, als ob er jeden Moment umkippen könnte, den Schlagzeuger hätte man glatt mit einem griesgrämigen Schalterbeamten verwechseln können, der Pianist hatte ein absolut festgeklebtes Grinsen, der Sänger hatte den Charme eines Kleiderständers und die Frau, die gesungen hat, erst…» Er schüttelte sich.

Una smiled. She didn't know what Manni was talking about, but she was sure it was about something he didn't like very much. Maybe he had had to follow the man into an expensive restaurant and had had to eat an oyster or something. She had eaten her first oyster recently and hadn't liked the experience at all. It had been so slimey. «Yuk», she shuddered, remembering it.

Manni sah Una verdutzt an. Sie versteht doch gar kein Deutsch, dachte er. Und reagiert so mitfühlend. Alle Achtung. «Und dann die Musik», fuhr er fort, «ich als ordentlicher Jazz-Rock-Fan muss mir da mit den Mumien zwei Stunden lang Musik zum Tanzen und Träumen reinziehen. Ehrlich, was man als Detektiv so alles durchmachen muss!»

«And was it worth it?», Sakina interrupted. She hadn't understood everything and didn't know what was wrong with music to dance and dream to.

«Ich glaub schon», antwortete Manni, «Andy Korbels Vater ist ganz am Ende aufgetaucht und er, Ginger Marley und der zweite Mann sind miteinander weggefahren. Ich hatte gedacht, Maddy, dass du vielleicht noch an ihm dranhingst.»

«Sorry, but I lost him almost immediately», Maddy sounded embarrassed. She began to tell Manni her story.

«Hey, stop a moment!», Una interrupted, «before everyone tells what happened to them again, I want to know what Manni just told you.» She thought she had been very patient. Sakina and Maddy did their best to sum it all up, asking Florian and Manni to clarify a lot of details as they went along.

Why didn't Manni like the music, Una asked herself, ‹popular melodies› could be nice. Didn't he have any taste? He dropped one point on her scale for that but gained it straight away for beeing so adventurous.

«Sag mal…» Manni fiel etwas ein, aber ein strafender Blick von Una ließ ihn die Sprache wechseln. «Tell me, what is a ‹bimbo›?» Henk und Florian schienen den Begriff nicht zu kennen. Florian dachte an einen großen Elefanten. Sakina, Maddy and Una looked at each other with expressions of embarrassment mixed with amusement. Una got up slowly and walked over to Manni, swinging her hips from side to side as she moved. «Just imagine, Manni», she said in high squeaky voice, «that I have long blonde hair, big blue eyes», she opened her eyes wide and fluttered her eyelashes, «and that all I want is for you to look after me, do all the thinking for me and pay for everything I do», she sat down on his knee and threw her arms around his shoulders, «then I'd be a bimbo», she squealed.

«Hm», sagte Manni, ziemlich verwirrt von Unas ungewöhnlicher Begriffserklärung, «is Ginger Marley a bimbo, then?»

That Una is a total flirt, Sakina thought annoyed. She looked at her Una as she got up from Manni's knee to go back to her seat. Henk and Florian were staring at her, too. Honestly!

Maddy answered Manni saying: «Maybe, why?»

Er erzählte ihnen, was er von den beiden Bühnenarbeitern gehört hatte. Wenn sie ein *bimbo* war und erst kurzfristig den Job als Gastgeberin für dieses Seniorenkonzert hatte, hieß das nicht, dass sie etwas wusste oder machte, wofür man sie belohnen musste? Was für eine Rolle spielte dabei der zweite Mann? Hatte er das Konzert produziert?

When Manni had said all this to the others, Una said sceptically: «If you were the hostess on a European television quiz show, why would you want to become the presenter of afternoon concerts for old folk?»

«It wasn't just a concert for old folk», Maddy corrected her, «it was a concert in the Queen Elizabeth Hall. That's quite a prestigious affair. It is probably very good for her career.»

Besser als 'ne Fernsehsendung?, dachte Florian ungläubig. «Look what Manni heard the stage-hands say about our quiz – it's kiddies' stuff», Maddy added, «I'm sure it's good for her career too, but the more different things she does the greater chance she probably has of really making it.»

«So where does all this leave us?», Sakina asked. She hadn't said anything for a quite while but had sat there listening to the others. No one answered her question. «Let me see now», she decided to take matters into her own hands, «what do we know so far? We know that there are definitely two Andys. The one who was there when the first show was recorded – Andy Korbel – wasn't on the recording when the show was broadcast. The Andy we saw on TV was Andy Hedley.»

Alle nickten. So viel stand auf jeden Fall fest.

«But when we ask about it in the studio», Sakina continued, «we are told it is just our imagination.»

«Dabei wissen die ganz genau, was Sache ist», fiel Florian ihr ins Wort, «schließlich muss es dort im Studio gemacht worden sein, das Vertauschen, meine ich.»

«Florian!», Una shouted impatiently.

«Sorry», he said and translated his last remark.

«Yes», exclaimed Una, «and now we know that Ginger Marley must be in on the plot if she knows Andy Korbel's father and the other man who got her the job in the posh hall.»

«Hold on», Henk butted in, «we don't know that for sure, yet.»

«It certainly looked like it when I was there», bestätigte Manni.

«Okay», sagte Florian, «but none of this tells us *why* it happened.»

Stille. Alle dachten nach. Nach einer Weile räusperte Henk sich und sagte: «One thing we do know for sure: Andy Korbel is still in London and walking around. That means that he has not disappeared or been kidnapped and that he is healthy and fit. So he wasn't cut out of the programme because he *couldn't* go on. His team's quarterfinal is being recorded tomorrow, so he could have been there.»

Maddy gave a long, low whistle. «Clever thinking, Henk», she praised him and then wished she hadn't when she saw a slow blush creeping over his face. He poked at his glasses with his finger and continued nevertheless: «That means that someone else didn't want him to be in the show. But who and why?» He paused. «From what Maddy, Manni and I saw today, we could speculate that it had something to do with the two men – the one who looked like Andy and who must be his father and the other one who Manni later saw with Ginger Marley.»

«I wonder», said Sakina slowly and with a thoughtful look on her face, «whether *that* is the clue to the whole affair.»

«Whether *what* is the clue?», shouted at least three voices at the same time.

«The fact that his father looks so much like him», Sakina said. «Maybe that's why he doesn't want Andy to be on television.»

Florian und Manni schauten sich fragend an, und auch bei

Maddy und Henk schien das Stirnrunzeln auf angestrengtes Nachdenken hinzuweisen. Only Una understood immediately what Sakina meant.

«I know», she screamed, «his father doesn't want his son to be seen on European television because he himself is a criminal!»

«Oh come on, Una!» Florian hielt das für eine ziemlich abwegige Idee.

«No, listen», she was serious. «Imagine the father was a Nazi or something like that who committed terrible crimes. He comes over to England after the war, changes his identity, and everything is okay. All of a sudden his son – who looks just like him – appears on European television and now people could find out where he is.»

«That's ridiculous», protestierte Manni.

Immer die bösen Deutschen, dachte Florian. Er hatte im MOMI heute schon genug von denen gehabt.

«Apart from the fact that it sounds unlikely», Henk said quietly, «I'd like to ask Una a history question: When did the Nazis commit their crimes? In the 1930s and 1940s. That means the father would have to be seventy or more today. The man we saw on the South Bank with Andy was nowhere near that age.»

Una shrugged her shoulders as if to show she thought it was an insignificant fact. «Well, it could be his grandfather, then», she muttered.

Mit Ausnahme von Manni redeten jetzt alle durcheinander. Manni hielt die Idee von dem Nazi-Opa auch für ziemlich weit hergeholt; aber irgendwas war an Sakinas und Unas Idee schon richtig, musste einfach richtig sein. Die Ähnlichkeit war verblüffend – warum sollte sie nicht der Grund gewesen sein? Vielleicht hatte der Vater im Ausland als Spion für den Geheimdienst gearbeitet, oder vielleicht arbeitete er jetzt immer noch dafür – würden da die Fernsehbilder nicht verraten, dass er Engländer ist?

«Shut up everyone for a minute», Maddy shouted to stop the noise. «Okay, so Una's idea is crazy, but it's a crazy situation when someone is cut out of a television recording. Does anyone have any other suggestions?» Manni probierte seine Idee an seinen Freunden aus. «Hmmm», Sakina commented, «if he was a spy who simply disappeared one day, he wouldn't want his son's face on the television to remind people of him or to give a clue about where he is now, would he? That makes sense.»

Maddy agreed. «And Manni, Henk and I overheard him on the terrace telling his son to trust him and to believe him. That would fit the picture, wouldn't it?»

«And where would that leave the second man on the terrace? What's his interest in the whole story?», Henk wanted to know.

«Maybe he's a friend of the father's and is helping him to organize the whole thing», Sakina suggested.

«Then he would have to be a spy, too. It's a bit much, isn't it?» Henk obviously wasn't convinced.

Florian rutschte erschöpft vom Sofa. Das stimmte alles hinten und vorne nicht. Das Einzige, was stimmte, war, dass was mit dem Andy nicht stimmte. Aber sonst? Nazis? Geheimdienst? Sie waren doch nicht im Kino. Nur im Fernsehen. Er sah die anderen an. Die sahen auch ziemlich erschöpft aus.

«I suppose tomorrow is another day, as my mother always says», Maddy finally spoke, «there's nothing more we can do today. But I think I'll take another look at the real Andy – Andy Korbel tomorrow.»

«I'll come along, too», sagte Florian.

«So will I», Una volunteered, «after all, you said you didn't think he was happy about the whole thing. If I do a Sakina on him maybe he'll crack up.» She emphasized the *I*. Sakina gave her a cold look. Silly cow, she thought. Das macht Una sicher gerne, dachte Florian. Bei den ersten Aufnahmen hatte sie schließlich gleich verkündet, der Andy erhalte ‹seven out of ten›. Wegen seiner schönen Augen.

Henk and Sakina arranged to meet in front of the local library. Henk asked Maddy for the photos. «What do you want them for?», Manni asked.

«Der hat nur einen *hunch*», klärte ihn Florian auf.

«Hä??»

«He's just got a vague idea or a feeling about something», Sakina threw in.

«Das hab ich auch», erklärte Manni, «mein *hunch* ist, dass ich morgen im Studio eine ganze Menge erfahren werde.»

«Die haben bestimmt schon alle *collywobbles*, weil du kommst», witzelte Florian. Manni zog verständnislos die Augenbrauen hoch.

The door opened. Mrs Butler came in. «Don't tell me you are all still learning for the quiz», she said. They all hesitated for a moment.

«Yes we are, Mum.» She turned to Una. «When did the Second World War take place?»

Una didn't answer. Instead she turned to Manni. «What is the name of the British Secret Service?»

Zehntes Kapitel

****

in dem Manni erkannt wird
and in which Charisma chops off a nose

«There you are, Manni, found your way alright, did you?», begrüßte ihn Derek.

«No problem», antwortete Manni, «is the rehearsal over?»
«Yes, no hitches today. Ready for your visit to the production people? You'll like it up there with them.» In diesem Augenblick kam Andy Hedley auf Derek zu. Als er Manni sah, stutzte er. Derek sah eine Sekunde lang verwirrt aus, dann stellte er ihn vor: «You two know each other already, don't you? Manni – Andy.» Andy stared at Manni, puzzled. «I don't think so», sagte er.

«No», sagte Manni. Was denkt Derek sich wohl dabei, fragte er sich.

«I must be confusing you with someone else. Let me see now», Derek dachte nach, «of course, Florian. It was Florian's team which played against Andy's in the Qualifying Round. How silly of me.»

Oder aber raffiniert. Wollte er damit zeigen, dass er wusste, dass sie hinter dem echten Andy her waren, oder war es wirklich nur eine Verwechslung? War das schon die erste Reaktion darauf, dass Sakina den zweiten Andy angemacht hatte? Er hatte keine Zeit, weiter darüber nachzudenken, denn Derek führte ihn in den Regieraum hinauf und *handed him over*, wie er das ausdrückte, an eine Frau, deren Namen er bei der Vorstellung nicht verstand. Das fing ja gut an.

«So, you are the kid who wants to look at how it's all done»,
sagte sie.

«Yes», sagte Manni. Von wegen *kid*.

«You know you'll have to keep very quiet. You can sit back
there.» Die Frau deutete auf einen Stuhl.

«Did you say you wanted to work in television or something
when you grow up?», fragte sie ihn, während sie an ihren Platz
zurückging.

«Yes, that would be nice», Manni ärgerte sich, dass seine
Antwort so nichtssagend klang. Aber wie die Frau mit ihm redete – *when you grow up* – als ob sie mit einem Dreikäsehoch
sprach.

«*That would be nice!* God, boys and girls», sagte sie zu ihren
Kollegen, «do you remember when we had those kind of illu-
sions about working for TV!» Alle lachten. Nur eine drehte
sich um:

«Aren't you the fellow who drew that lovely cuckoo clock in
the nest?», fragte sie Manni.

Er freute sich, dass wenigstens eine ihn halbwegs ernst nahm
und sich an seine Glanzstunde erinnerte. «Yes, that was me»,
sagte er.

«What was your name again?»

«Manni – I'm from Berlin», fügte er hinzu.

Vor den Leuten, die in diesem Raum, den sie die *gallery*
nannten, arbeiteten, war eine Wand voller Bildschirme. Fünf
von ihnen, die nummeriert waren, zeigten gerade jeweils das,
was jede der fünf Kameras im Studio einfing. Ein paar zeigten
im Moment gar nichts, ein weiterer sah wie ein Computer-
Bildschirm aus, auf dem gerade ein Programm lief, mit dem
man Text in die Show einblenden konnte – damit arbeitete die
Frau, die Manni in Empfang genommen hatte. Und auf wie-

der zwei anderen Bildschirmen liefen jeweils Aufnahmen von der SUPERCHAIN-Sendung, die am Vortag aufgenommen worden war. Warum läuft das Band gerade jetzt? Ich müsste jemandem ein paar Fragen stellen können, dachte er.

«Okay everybody?», sagte der Mann, von dem Manni inzwischen glaubte, dass er der Regisseur war, ins Mikrofon. Während alle anderen in der *gallery* entweder riesige Mischpulte, Computer-Keyboards oder irgendwelche Knöpfe vor sich hatten, an denen sie ständig rumfummelten, hatte er nur dieses Mikrofon und redete ständig mit den Leuten im Studio. Dort unten trugen fast alle Kopfhörer und viele auch ein Mikrofon. Die waren wohl in ständigem Kontakt mit der *gallery*. «We are on talkback», hatte Joanne das genannt. Manni hatte schon mitbekommen, wie sie manchmal unten nervös wurden, während der Regisseur mit ihnen sprach. Nun konnte Manni hören, was er den Leuten alles sagte.

Auf einmal war es so weit. Alle schienen sich plötzlich zu konzentrieren.

«Stand by studio», sagte der Regisseur ruhig, «stand by lights, stand by sound, stand by VT… go VT.»

«Thirty seconds», sagte die Frau mit der Stoppuhr in der Hand in ihr Mikrofon, «twenty seconds… ten, nine, eight.»

«Stand by camera 3», rief der Regisseur dazwischen.

«…two, one, zero.»

«Go, music… go», befahl der Regisseur, «lighting change one, lighting change two, mix to three, coming to camera 2 next…»

Manni hörte sein Herz schlagen. Alles geschah so schnell und viele Stimmen redeten durcheinander. Die Eröffnungsfanfare ertönte.

«Go revolve» – die Dekoration öffnete sich und drehte die

Kandidaten ins Blickfeld. «Ladies and gentlemen, welcome your hostess, Ginger Marley», kam die Stimme vom Band. «Ready with the winner board, VT?», fragte der Regisseur übers *talkback*, «ready Charisma?», fragte er den Mann, der neben ihm saß. Komischer Name für einen Mann, dachte Manni, während Ginger ihren Eröffnungsspruch ablas. «Run VT.» Der Regisseur klang weiterhin ganz ruhig.

«My, we are looking chic today», kommentierte die Textverarbeitungsfrau gehässig Gingers Kleid.

Da oben in der *gallery* kam es Manni fast vor, als ob das, was unten im Studio mit den Kandidaten geschah, völlig nebensächlich war. Es schien egal zu sein, was sie und Ginger Marley machten, Hauptsache alle Kameras waren auf dem richtigen Platz mit der richtigen Einstellung, und Bild und Ton kamen zum richtigen Moment und mit der richtigen Lautstärke. Dass das alles so kompliziert war, hätte er sich nicht gedacht.

«Camera 1, where are you?», fragte der Regisseur verärgert; der Bildschirm für Kamera 1 war total verschwommen.

«Soory, Bill», kam es zurück, «something's wrong with the camera.»

«Okay, nothing you can do about it», sagte der Regisseur erstaunlich gleichmütig, wie Manni fand, «stop VT, stop everybody.»

Charisma, der Mann, der neben dem Regisseur saß, zündete sich eine Zigarette an und spielte mit seinem Computer. Es war unglaublich, was er mit dieser Maschine alles machen konnte. Manni konnte gerade über seine Schultern sehen. Er zeichnete einen Kasten, der in sich selber verschwand, er machte wahnsinnige dreidimensionale geometrische Formen und spielte auch mit den Kamerabildern herum. Gerade gab es eine Großaufnahme von Carla aus Dänemark auf Kamera 3. Manni wusste nicht, wie er es machte, aber es war, als ob Charisma Carlas Nase herausschnitt und dann wieder anklebte, bloß andersrum. Irre komisch sah es aus. Manni musste lachen. Der Mann drehte sich um. «I'll bet you haven't seen a Charisma machine before, eh?»

«No, I haven't», gab Manni zu, und war froh, dass er den Mann noch nicht mit ‹Charisma› angeredet hatte, «can you change whole pictures with it?», fragte er schnell. Jetzt, wo jemand mit ihm redete, wollte er wenigstens was herausfinden. Aber bevor er eine Antwort erhielt, ging die Tür auf, und ein Mann steckte seinen Kopf ins Zimmer. «Got a second, Bill?», sagte er in einem Ton, der kaum Widerspruch zuließ.

«Sure», antwortete der Regisseur und verließ den Raum. Manni wurde ganz heiß und schwarz vor Augen. Gut, dass er saß. Es gab keinen Zweifel: Das war der zweite Mann gewesen, der, den er am Vortag beschattet hatte.

«What an honour», sagte die Frau, die den Text eintippte, «God himself coming to visit us.» Manni musste wohl ein ziemlich verwirrtes Gesicht gemacht haben, denn die nette Frau, die, die ihn gleich erkannt hatte, erklärte ihm:

«That's Stephen Robinson. You might have seen his name on the credits at the end of the show. The last three names on them are the director – that's Bill who's just gone out –, the producer Tamara Jones who sits next door, and at the very end it says ‹Executive Producer: Stephen Robinson› – that's him. Responsible for everything and nothing. But he doesn't usually come in for the normal recordings, he's mostly off jetting around the world buying new shoes and stuff.»

«That's very interesting, thanks», antwortete Manni, der seine Fassung wieder gefunden hatte. In seinem Kopf arbeitete es fieberhaft. Stephen Robinson? Stephen Robinson? Richtig!

Hatte bei dem entsetzlichen Konzert gestern nicht im Programmheft gestanden *A Stephen Robinson Production*? Oder bildete er sich das nur ein? Er konnte jetzt nicht einfach sitzen bleiben und warten.

«Excuse me, eh...», wandte er sich wieder an die Frau.

«Wendy», antwortete die, «my name is Wendy.»

«Excuse me, Wendy, could you tell me where the... em... where the toilets are?»

Wendy smiled. «Go out the door, turn right and go down the stairs. It's the first door on the left, okay?»

«Thanks», sagte Manni und stand auf. Gott sei Dank, *turn right* war in die Richtung, in die auch der Regisseur verschwunden war.

Manni musste nicht weit gehen. Gleich durch die nächste Glastür sah er Stephen Robinson, Ginger Marley, Bill, den Regisseur, und noch eine Frau, das war bestimmt Tamara Jones, die Produzentin der Sendung. Sie redeten heftig aufeinander ein. Schade, dass im Studio alle Räume schalldicht waren.

«Hi, Manni, everything okay?»

Manni fuhr zusammen. Hinter ihm stand Derek, der gerade die Treppe heraufgekommen war.

«Oh yes, fine thanks, I'm just on my way to the toilet.»

«Then don't let me keep you. You know the way?»

Manni nickte und ging weiter. Als er sich umdrehte, sah er, wie Derek gerade in das Zimmer der Produzentin hineinging.

Maddy, Una and Florian took it in turns to keep an eye on Andy Korbel's house. All three of them hanging around near it would have looked too suspicious. Nothing happened for a long time. Florian hatte schon zweimal vorgeschlagen, lieber irgendetwas anzustellen, als nur blöd herumzuhängen, als

Andy endlich aus dem Haus trat, Walkman im Ohr. Er schien eine Weile ziellos durch den nächsten Park zu laufen. Dann setzte er sich, öffnete seinen Walkman, holte aus seiner Tasche eine CD heraus und wechselte die Platte.

«Ich werd nicht mehr, ein CD-Walkman – ein Discman!», rief Florian neidisch, «so was möchte ich auch haben! Sein Alter hat bestimmt massenweise Knete. Ein *rich kid*, aber echt mal.» Maddy laughed. Florian calling somebody else a rich kid was good, she thought. «Maybe he bought it himself», she suggested, «maybe he has a job somewhere, who knows?»

«Hmm», grummelte Florian.

Una couldn't follow what Florian was saying. From what I can hear he doesn't seem to be very happy about whatever it is that's going on, she thought. Maybe it was time she did a Sakina on Andy. After all, she had liked the look of him in the studio.

Auf dem Rückweg von der Toilette machte Manni eine Tür auf, die rechts vom Flur abging. Solange ich hier bei der Technik bin, will ich so viel wie möglich sehen, sagte er sich. Zwei Männer und eine Frau saßen vor zwei Bildschirmen. Es handelte sich dabei wohl nicht um normale Bildschirme. Oben sah man die Bilder und unten auf dem gleichen Gerät waren unendlich viele Knöpfe und Hebel. Einer der beiden Männer arbeitete gerade an einem dieser Geräte. Der andere und die Frau drehten sich um, als Manni hereinkam.

«Well, well, what have we got here», sagte die Frau. Sie hatte eine freundliche Stimme. «Lost your way, then?» – «No», sagte Manni, «I am having a look at the technical side of television making today. I was in the gallery and now I'm looking around.» Das klingt bestimmt sehr professionell, wie ich da von der *gallery* rede, sagte er sich.

«You are in one of the teams, aren't you?», fragte der Mann.

«Yes, the Floppies», antwortete Manni, «my name is Manni, I'm from Berlin.»

«Hi, Manni, we're the VT people.»

Toll! Manni wollte schon die ganze Zeit herausfinden, was die VT-Leute eigentlich genau waren und machten. Und die drei sahen so aus, als ob man sie was fragen könnte.

«VT», erklärte die Frau, «stands for video tape. That's what the show is recorded on. We are the most important people for the recording – all the elements come together here, we do all the editing and everything.»

Hieß das, dass die beiden Andys hier vertauscht worden waren? Das fragte Manni natürlich nicht. Ihm fiel etwas anderes ein:

«If something goes wrong during the recording – say Ginger makes a mistake when she announces the scores and that bit is recorded again, with her saying the proper scores – is the old wrong piece cut out of the tape and the new piece stuck in?»

«You want to know about that?», fragte der Mann.

Hoffentlich schöpft er keinen Verdacht, dachte Manni, aber es ist doch eigentlich natürlich, dass einen so was interessiert. «Yes, please», sagte er mit unschuldiger Miene.

«Well, we don't physically cut anything out of the tape, we do what we call ‹dropping in› a shot. When the show is finished, we run the tape to the part where the mistake is, run another tape which has the correct shot, and record the new shot over the old one. The new drop-in shot has to be the same length as the old one and it has to match the beginning and end of the old shot.»

Interessant, dachte Manni. So war der falsche Andy also in die Show gekommen.

«It is the cheapest and fastest way of editing», fuhr der Mann fort, «and that's why we have the two machines here – we run them both and record from one to the other.»

«Fascinating!», sagte Manni und meinte es auch so. «And how long or short can these drop-ins be?», fragte er weiter.

«For every second there are twenty-five frames – for each second you watch on TV that is. We can replace every single one of them, frame by frame», erklärte der Mann, der sichtlich stolz auf seine Maschine war.

«Amazing», sagte Manni, «simply amazing. I've learnt a lot here today, thank you», bedankte er sich.

Als er gerade in den Regieraum zurückgehen wollte, kam Stephen Robinson aus dem Zimmer der Produzentin.

«Hey», sprach er Manni an, «haven't I seen you somewhere before?»

Manni bekam ganz weiche Knie. Natürlich hat er mich schon mal gesehen, dachte er, gestern, als Maddy das Foto von mir gemacht hat. Und siedend heiß durchfuhr es ihn: ob er mich auch noch in der Queen Elizabeth Hall erkannt hat? Manni war von sich selbst sehr beeindruckt, als er sich ganz ruhig antworten hörte: «Oh yes, I am a member of the Floppies team, we won our quarterfinal the day before yesterday. You must have seen me in the studio. My name is Manni.»

Stephen Robinson schien ihn einen Augenblick lang durchdringend zu mustern, dann lächelte er und sagte: «Of course. Yes, I was here on Tuesday. You are the one who wants to work in television one day so you're having a look at the technical side of the show today. Bill told me about that.»

Manni nickte.

«Well, that's great. Television always needs good people to work behind the camera. Enjoy yourself», sagte er freundlich, während er zur Treppe ging. Manni war schweißgebadet, als er wieder auf seinem Stuhl hinten im Regieraum saß. Und dabei war es doch angeblich nur im Licht der Scheinwerfer bei den Aufnahmen heiß. Schnell nahm ihn die Atmosphäre im Regieraum wieder gefangen.

«Thirty seconds», sagte die Frau mit der Stoppuhr in der Hand gerade ins Mikrofon.

Chapter eleven

****

in which Una does a Sakina
und in dem zwei Bücherwürmer Erfolg haben

«Andy, what a coincidence!» Una ran over to the bench where Andy Korbel was sitting and planted a big kiss on his cheek. Der arme Bursche sah total verblüfft aus. Im Studio hatten sie zwar ein bisschen miteinander geflirtet, das hatte auch Florian mitgekriegt, aber so nah waren sie einander doch nicht gekommen, oder? Der Blick auf Andys Gesicht schien das zu bestätigen.

«Imagine just meeting you here like this!», Una continued, «how are you?»

«Fine, thanks», said Andy quietly.

«Look, Florian is here too, and Maddy – she belongs to one of the other teams, the Floppies», Una explained as she waved them over.

«Hallo», sagte Florian. Mehr fiel ihm nicht ein.

Vielleicht hätten sie vorher einen Plan machen sollen, statt einfach nur aufzukreuzen. Aber Una schien zu wissen, was sie wollte.

«Aren't you supposed to be in the studio?», Una asked Andy, «I thought the Argonauts had their quarterfinal today.»

Andy war plötzlich mit den Knöpfen seines Walkmans beschäftigt und sah sie nicht an. «Em… I'm not sure», murmelte er.

«Not sure!», Una screamed, «maybe they are all sitting

there, waiting for you to turn up. Didn't Derek or Joanne get in touch with you?»

«No», er war kaum hörbar. Er tat Florian richtig Leid. Offensichtlich wusste er überhaupt nicht, was er sagen sollte.

Andy stand plötzlich auf. «Look, I have to go. I'll see you again sometime, okay?», sagte er und wollte gehen. Una put her hand on his arm and said in gentle voice: «You aren't in the quiz any more, are you, Andy? We saw the show on TV – our show – and you weren't in it. What's happening?»

«I don't know what you are talking about», versuchte er zu bluffen, «leave me alone.» Wieder versuchte er sich loszureißen.

«We know that Andy Hedley has taken your place in the Argonauts and we want to know why. If you won't help us then we'll have to find out without you», stieg Florian ein.

Andy ließ sich auf die Bank fallen. Er kämpfte mit den Tränen. «Okay», sagte er resigniert, «I'll tell you what I know but please don't make any trouble. It's bad enough as it is.»

Andy erzählte, dass er sich zusammen mit seinen Freunden David und Carla um einen Platz als Mannschaft für SUPER-CHAIN beworben hatte – genau wie die Jugglers und die Floppies. Die drei hatten sich zusammen darauf vorbereitet. Und dann kam das erste Ausscheidungsspiel. Es hatte ihnen sehr viel Spaß gemacht. «Especially when we won», he said and gave a weak smile.

Florian ließ es sich nicht nehmen zu sagen: «Well you didn't knock us out, you know, we won the Consolation Match against the Jitterbugs on Monday.»

«I'm glad to hear it», said Andy. He was a little more relaxed now as he continued with his story.

«The evening after the recording my father came home early

for a change so I actually got to talk to him. You see I rarely see him because he is always away on business. He travels all over the world. I told him about the day in the studio and how we had won. He seemed to be pleased about it and asked me what kind of a quiz it was. When he heard that it was going to be shown in the whole of Europe on satellite TV he went totally crazy. I've never seen him like that before.» Andy schüttelte den Kopf, als ob er diese Reaktion immer noch nicht verstand. Auch Florian, Maddy und Una hatten keine Idee, warum jemand so reagieren würde.

Andy continued: «He started shouting at me, asking why I hadn't asked his permission first and that he'd soon show me the consequences of my actions. I thought he had gone out of his mind.»

Andy erzählte, wie sein Vater ihn auf sein Zimmer geschickt und telefoniert hatte. Eine Weile später war er zu ihm gekommen und hatte gesagt, dass alles wieder gut sei. «He said I should just imagine I had never been involved in the first place and asked me for my friend Andy Hedley's phone number. Andy told me later that he was asked to take my place in the quiz and that he was told that things could be difficult for me if he didn't.» Wieso würde es für ihn schwierig werden, wollte Florian wissen. Andy wusste darauf keine Antwort.

«And why didn't your father want you to be on television in Europe?», Maddy asked.

Andy paused. «If only I knew. I keep asking him why, but he says he can't tell me and if I make a fuss, things could be difficult for him.»

Ein bisschen viel *difficulty*, dachte Florian.

«I've asked him over and over again», Andy continued, «and all he keeps saying is that I have to believe him when he says he could be put in a very difficult position. And that I should trust him. He thinks I'm still a kid who can be told what to do», he concluded angrily.

«And what about the other man who was with you and your father on the South Bank yesterday?», Maddy asked.

Andy sah sie total verblüfft an. «What?»

Mensch, Maddy, dachte Florian. Du und deine große Klappe. Der weiß doch gar nicht, dass wir ihn gestern beschattet haben.

Andy turned to Una. «So meeting you here wasn't really a coincidence, was it?» He looked each of them in the face. «You really do want to find out what this is about, don't you?»

Sie nickten.

«Well, so do I», he said, «but I am afraid that my father is right and that we'll make trouble if we ask too many questions.»

«But I thought he just wanted to make sure you weren't on European television. Now that you aren't, surely no great damage can be done», Una speculated.

Andy überlegte einen Moment. «Maybe you are right», sagte er, «I just don't know.»

Eigentlich müsste man ihn jetzt direkt ins Studio bringen und sehen, was passiert, dachte Florian. Aber dabei würde Andy wohl nicht mitspielen. ‹Nicht› oder ‹noch nicht›?

«Look», Maddy said, «I'll give you my phone number, just in case.»

Es war ein spannendes Spiel. Die Argonauts führten nach der ersten Runde 3 : 2, aber sie waren beim Spielen und Zeichnen in der zweiten Runde voll von der Rolle, sodass die Tigers mit 4 : 3 in Führung gingen. Auch in der dritten Runde verteidigten sie ihren knappen Vorsprung. Aber in der *gallery* oben war das Hin und Her im Spiel anscheinend ohne Bedeutung: jeder war vollauf damit beschäftigt, die richtigen Bilder und Töne einzufangen.

«Camera 2, line up a shot of the general knowledge candidate», kam die Anweisung von Bill.

«I'll take the risk question», sagte David aus Edinburgh. «I thought you might», Ginger Marley schenkte ihm ihr breites Lächeln. «Well, David, in 1989 the people of East Berlin were allowed for the first time since the wall was built to cross the border into West Berlin. In which month did it happen?»

Mann, dachte Manni, das soll 'ne Risikofrage sein? Das ist doch kinderleicht. Er war schließlich am 9. November kurz nach Mitternacht mit seinen Eltern auf den Ku'damm gegangen und hatte mit all den Ossis gefeiert. Irre war das gewesen. Noch heute lief es ihm kalt den Rücken hinunter, als er daran dachte. Und dann das Wochenende danach! Die Massen in der U-Bahn, alle gutmütig, die Geschäfte, die Ostgeld nahmen, die langen Schlangen für das Begrüßungsgeld und der kleine Unfall an der Ecke, wo ein Trabi und ein Mercedes sich gestreift hatten und der Mercedes-Fahrer ausgestiegen war und den Trabi-Fahrer per Handschlag freundlich begrüßt hatte. Und das Spiel von Hertha BSC am Samstag, wo all die Ostler freien Eintritt hatten und eine Riesenstimmung herrschte.

«That's a difficult one, alright», riss ihn eine Bemerkung des Charisma-Mannes aus seinen Erinnerungen. Und auch David schien Schwierigkeiten zu haben.

«October?», sagte er schließlich.

«Oh, hard luck, David», Ginger Marleys Stimme triefte vor Mitleid, «you just missed it by one month. Well, risk *questions* can be very difficult, I did warn you.»

Die Frage hätten sie mir mal geben sollen, dachte Manni; Monat und Tag hätte ich nennen können, auch in hundert Jahren noch.

Während Mannis Gedanken an den Potsdamer Platz zurückkehrten, wo er am Sonntag, halb zerquetscht von den anderen Schaulustigen, dabei war, als dort ein Loch in die Mauer geschlagen wurde, machten die Argonauts Boden gut. 8 : 7 gewannen sie am Ende.

«What an exciting finish», rief Ginger Marley aus, «a low scoring game, but the Argonauts are now in the semifinal. One step nearer to Florida. We'll see them again, but we have to say goodbye to the Tigers…»

Während sich Ginger Marley auch von den Zuschauern verabschiedete, schlich sich Manni aus dem Regieraum, ging leise und ganz langsam die Treppe hinunter und mit äußerster Vorsicht hinter die Dekoration in Richtung Ausgang des Studios. Derek und Joanne hatten allen Kandidaten zwar tausendmal gesagt, niemand dürfe sich von seinem Platz entfernen, während die Aufnahmen liefen, denn man könnte ins Bild geraten oder Krach machen, und dann müsste neu aufgenommen werden, aber er wollte unbedingt am Ausgang sein, bevor die Argonauts verschwanden.

Als der Applaus vorbei war und der Aufnahmeleiter das *all clear* gegeben hatte, ging Manni ins Studio hinein. «Congratulations», sagte er zu Carla, David und Andy, die mit Derek zusammenstanden, «that was great. It won't be easy for us if we have to play against you in the semifinal.» Andy lachte unsicher. «But then I suppose Sakina's team wouldn't have an easy time against you either. I hear she was very impressed by you when you played against the Jugglers in the Qualifying Round.» Das Lächeln verschwand aus Andys Gesicht.

«That was a clever thing to say to him», Una remarked when they all met again in the evening and Manni told them about his day, «it will confuse him even more.»

«Well», antwortete Manni, sehr mit sich zufrieden, «Henk said yesterday that Sakina had set a cat amongst the pigeons. Now I have thrown in a second one.»

Florian, Maddy und Una erzählten dann von ihrer Begegnung mit Andy im Park. Der arme Kerl, dachte Manni, was immer dahinter steckt, der ist auf jeden Fall in einer miesen Situation. Manni fiel auf, dass Henk und Sakina überhaupt noch nichts gesagt hatten. «Well, Mr and Mrs Bookworm», sagte er, «did you have a nice day in the library?»

Sakina smiled at Henk, Henk blushed a little and then took a photocopy out of his pocket. «A very nice day indeed», he said and showed it to them. «It's from *Who's Who in the Media in Britain.*»

Einen 1929 geborenen Prof. Anthony Korbel gab es da, dessen Hauptwerk ‹Soap Opera and the Viewer› hieß. Und in London einen Gary Korbel.

«He was born in London 1942», Sakina gave a summary of the long entry. «After graduating from Oxford in 1964, he worked as a journalist on a major London newspaper and made his fortune in Australia in the late 1970s by setting up several successful film production companies and investing into cable and satellite TV. He has bought the newspaper on which he had previously worked and several English and American production companies and is one of the really big media men. He is now based in London.»

«Phew», Una said, «that must be our man.»

Manni wollte wissen, ob der Artikel ein Foto von ihm enthielt.

«No», Sakina said, «that's what is odd about it. There was a photo of most of the people in that book – people who are much less important than he is. But there was none of him.»

Zwölftes Kapital

****

in dem Florian einen irischen Heiligen unterschätzt
and in which Una's skill is put to the test

Florian gähnte. Wie an jedem anderen Tag auch fanden am Vormittag Proben statt, bei denen die Produktionsassistentin Rosemary die Rolle von Ginger Marley übernahm. Rosemary stellte gerade einer Spanierin von den Cyclists eine Frage.

«Tired?», asked Una.

«Yeah», antwortete Florian leise, «but I was just thinking how clever Henk was to have found the information he told us about last night.»

«Hey! Just a minute», Sakina hissed, taking care nobody heard what she was saying, «Henk and I both found that information. If I hadn't known the local libraries so well, we wouldn't have found anything.»

Bei den Proben ging heute aber auch alles schief. Das lag nicht an den Jugglers und den Cyclists, die die Spielregeln inzwischen wirklich auswendig konnten, sondern an der Technik. Komisch, dachte Florian, die machen das jeden Tag, proben auch jeden Morgen, und dann gibt's doch Tage, an denen alles schief läuft.

«Heard anything yet, love», hörte er den Mann an der Kamera 2 zu Rosemary sagen, während das ganze Studio darauf wartete, dass die Drehbühne sich wieder drehen ließ: Sie hatte sich festgeklemmt.

Rosemary sah sich um, als ob sie fürchtete, dass ihr jemand

zuhören könnte, und sagte dann halblaut: «I've sent three copies away to different production companies, but I haven't heard anything yet. I still have another three which I'll send off soon. Nobody is supposed to know about it so you and VT should keep your mouths shut.»

«*Nobody* meaning her Royal Marley Highness, I suppose», lachte der Kameramann.

«Well, it is her show», antwortete Rosemary und ging in die Dekoration zurück, die inzwischen wieder beweglich war.

Worum es dabei wohl ging, fragte sich Florian. Hatten die anderen das auch mitbekommen? Una flirtete gerade mit Lars von den Cyclists. Das Mädchen ist unglaublich, dachte Florian, wahrscheinlich überlegt sie gleichzeitig dabei, wie viel Punkte er bekommen soll. Sakina had heard the conversation between Rosemary and the cameraman as well and was wondering what it was about. What kind of copies had Rosemary sent away and why shouldn't Ginger Marley find out about them? Sakina didn't have much time to speculate any further. The rehearsal was about to continue.

In der nächsten Pause standen Florian und Sakina in der Kaffeeschlange direkt hinter Rosemary, ohne das vorher geplant zu haben. «Rosemary», said Sakina, «you know, you ask the *questions* really well in the rehearsal.»

«Oh, thank you, Sakina», said Rosemary, obviously pleased.

«And you look very good on the screen, too», Florian buttered her up.

«Well, it's nice to know I have two fans. A black coffee, please», she said to the coffee lady.

«Did you ever think of becoming a quiz show hostess?», Sakina asked innocently, «you could do Ginger Marley's job just as well as she does.» Nicht so schnell, dachte Florian. Nicht so direkt. Rosemary sah sich um, so als ob sie sich ertappt fühlte, aber da hinter ihnen niemand stand, sagte sie:

«You shouldn't let Ginger hear you say that, she wouldn't like it at all. But yes, as a matter of fact, I would like to be a quiz show hostess.»

Florian und Sakina hatten inzwischen auch etwas zu trinken erhalten und folgten Rosemary an einen Tisch. «How do you become one – a quiz show hostess, I mean», Sakina persisted.

«Well, you have to get in touch with different production companies who make quizzes and let them have a sample of your work.»

«But how can you do that if you are not working as a one already?» Sakina didn't let up.

Na, dachte Florian, was kommt denn jetzt? Rosemary sah sich wieder um und sagte dann halb verschwörerisch: «Keep this to yourselves and don't tell anybody – promise?» Sakina und Florian nickten ernsthaft, so ernsthaft, wie sie nur konnten.

Rosemary erzählte, dass einer der VT-Männer, mit dem sie sehr gut auskam, sie bei einer der ersten Proben aufgenommen und das Material so zusammengestellt hatte, dass es fast so gut wie eine echte Sendung aussah. «It was wonderful of him, really», schwärmte Rosemary, «otherwise I would never have had a chance of making a demo tape.»

«And have you sent it away, yet?», asked Sakina, even though she knew the answer.

«Yes. I got several copies made and have sent some away.»

«And who are the lucky contestants who are on the tape?», fragte Florian ganz nebensächlich.

«Funny you should ask, Florian. It is Sakina's and your

team. It was one of the very first rehearsals. And very nice the two of you look on it, too.»

Florian verschluckte sich fast an seinem Getränk. Er hustete, bis ihm die Tränen kamen.

Sakina thumped Florian's back and said to Rosemary: «I think, Florian needs a bit of fresh air. Good luck with the production companies. We won't say a word to anyone.» She pulled him by the arm and they walked away.

Sie suchten nach Una. Die saß mit Lars zusammen. Sie zogen sie weg und erzählten schnell, was sie in dem Studio gehört hatten und was Rosemary in der letzten Pause gesagt hatte.

Una looked at them. «You mean... you think she might have a tape with... my God!» Una seemed to be almost lost for words. «Yes, Sakina assured her, «if it is a rehearsal tape of one of the earliest episodes with us on it, then the Argonauts with Andy Korbel must be on it, too.»

«My God!» Una was still lost for words.

«We have to decide what to do», drängelte Florian. «The question is, how can we get our hands on it?»

Una thought for a moment. «You said she had another three copies which she hasn't sent away yet. Maybe she has them here in the studio in her bag or her locker or somewhere.»

«And if we do find a copy? What then?», asked Sakina anxiously.

«Well, we'll sort of borrow it, of course, won't we?», replied Una.

«Why don't you tell us a bit about yourselves?», Ginger Marley said to the contestants in the afternoon when they were between rounds. She smiled into the camera: «I'm sure the people at home would like to get to know you better.»

Von wegen besser kennen lernen, dachte Florian. Er hatte gesehen, wie der Aufnahmeleiter hinter der Kamera Ginger gerade ein Zeichen gemacht hatte. Es sah so aus, als würde er mit den Daumen und Zeigefingern einen Kaugummi auseinander ziehen. Er zeigte ihr an, dass die Sendung bis jetzt unter der geplanten Zeit lag und dass sie mit *smalltalk* den Beginn der nächsten Runde etwas hinauszögern sollte.

«Una. Let me see now… if I remember rightly you told us the first week you were here that you have two sisters and one brother and that you sang in a choir in Dublin», Ginger said.

Die Zuschauer denken sicher, dass sie sich das alles gemerkt hat, fuhr es Florian durch den Kopf, dabei las sie alles von der *cue card* ab, die eine Assistentin hinter der Kamera hochhielt.

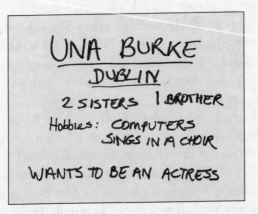

UNA BURKE
DUBLIN
2 SISTERS 1 BROTHER
Hobbies: COMPUTERS
        SINGS IN A CHOIR

WANTS TO BE AN ACTRESS

«We've had quite a few musical contestants so far», Ginger Marley continued. «A few weeks ago we had someone who played the trumpet. Let me think now, a young German I think, yes – Manni Hutzner. From Berlin, just like Florian.

It's nice to see so much interest amongst young people for music.»

Florian wurde es ganz mulmig. Das mit Manni und seiner Trompete und Berlin stand gerade nicht auf der *cue card*. Und per Zufall merkte sich diese Medien-Dame bestimmt nichts. Wollte sie damit zeigen, dass sie wusste, dass die Jugglers mit den Floppies unter einem Hut steckten und zusammen an der Andy-Geschichte dran waren? Florian verscheuchte den Gedanken. Er musste sich auf das Spiel konzentrieren. Nach der ersten Runde stand es 3 : 3 zwischen den Cyclists und den Jugglers.

The film title which had to be mimed, drawn and guessed in Round 2 was ‹Gorillas in the Mist›. Unfortunately Sakina had never heard of it. The audience fell about with laughter when Una did her gorilla act, and Sakina guessed that part quickly. It was the ‹mist› which she couldn't guess. She was in agony till the time was over. No link for the Floppies in that round. Their opponents had only just finished in time so they got one link for winning – but they didn't get any of the bonus links going for speed.

Trotzdem gab es nach der Runde tosenden Beifall. Florian blickte skeptisch in Richtung Zuschauer. Es waren heute nicht gerade viele da. Eine Schulklasse, die wahrscheinlich gerade ein Projekt über Medien machte, ein paar Interessierte und die übliche Busladung aus einem Altersheim. Der Besuch im Fernsehstudio war wahrscheinlich der kulturelle Höhepunkt der Woche. Einige waren ganz begeistert. Andere saßen teilnahmslos da und starrten vor sich hin. Wieder andere schliefen. Was für ein Leben. Florian nahm sich vor, seiner Oma eine Postkarte aus London zu schicken. Eigentlich sollte er ihr öfters schreiben und sie besuchen und überhaupt… Na ja, immerhin

würde sie ihn jetzt ein paar Mal im Fernsehen bewundern können. Das würde sie bestimmt freuen.

«I think coffee is going to come out of my ears soon», Una
complained during the break after Round 2 as she cut off a
corner of Florian's cake and popped it into her mouth. «We
seem to spend more time sitting around drinking the stuff than
we spend in the studio.»

Bitte nimm doch, Una, knurrte Florian in sich hinein. Wenn
sie bloß vorher fragen würde, bevor sie in seinem Kuchen her-
umstocherte. Dabei sagte sie ständig, sie wolle keinen haben.
Obwohl Florian und Sakina eigentlich allein mit ihr reden
wollten, waren die drei an einem Tisch mit Brendan, einem der
Tontechniker, gelandet. «That's the secret of television», said
Brendan, «sitting around drinking coffee.»

Er war einer der wenigen Leute von der Technik, die während der Pause auch mal einen Kaffee mit den Kandidaten tranken. Ein freundlicher Typ. Er hatte ein Glasauge und sagte von
sich: «Most people have two eyes and two ears. I only have one
proper eye but in place of the other one I have a third ear. Very
useful for a sound technician.»

«Can I ask you a question, Brendan?», fragte Florian.

«Fire ahead.»

Florian erzählte, dass ihm aufgefallen war, dass verhältnis-
mäßig wenig Leute im Zuschauerraum waren, aber trotzdem
viel Applaus zu hören war. Wie das denn käme? «A real smart
lad, this Florian here», Brendan winked with his glass eye at
Una, «he wants to find out all the tricks of the trade. Okay, I'll
tell you how it's done. We call it ‹tracking up the applause›.»

Florian konnte sich vorstellen, dass Leute von der Technik
leicht an jemandem, der nicht viel Ahnung hatte, vorbeierklä-
ren konnten. Bei Brendan aber war das anders. Er fing dort an,

wo Florian ihm leicht folgen konnte, und am Ende hatte er eine brauchbare Erklärung gegeben. Wenn nur wenige Zuschauer da waren, konnte der Beifall technisch verstärkt werden, sodass man den Eindruck hatte, dass das Haus voll war. Das Geklatsche wurde einfach vervielfacht. Das machten sie in Brendans Abteilung ‹Sound›.

«The warm-up man has to warn the audience when we are going to track up their sound», Brendan explained. «It's okay having one person's applause sounding like sixteen people clapping, but if they cough or talk to their neighbour during the show then you have that sixteen times louder, too.»

Faszinierend, was man so alles mit der Technik machen kann, dachte Florian. Und am letzten Sonntag hatte er noch geglaubt, dass man unmöglich den ersten Andy irgendwie aus der Aufnahme herausnehmen und durch einen anderen ersetzen konnte. Er wollte aber Brendan nicht darauf ansprechen. Noch nicht.

«Here's looking at you, kids», sagte der, als er mit dem Glas Wasser, das er zu seinem Kaffee trank, gegen sein Auge stieß. Glas gegen Glas.

Una, Sakina and Florian must have been on the same wavelength that day. Their performance in the true/false round was terrific. In four out of the five statements that were made, they were right when they all decided that they were either false or true. The only one that didn't work was their reaction to the statement «The horse-drawn carriages known as *Fiaker* in Austria, *fiacre* in France and *fiaccero* in Italy got their name from the picture of the Irish Saint Fiacre painted on the wall of the house in Paris outside which the first ones parked.» Una liked the sound of it and went for her ‹true› button straight away. Die Iren und ihre Heiligen, dachte Florian, sie wollen sie überall wieder finden. Er war vor einem Jahr in Wien gewesen und war sich sicher, dass Fiaker bestimmt nichts mit irgendeinem Iren zu tun hat. Er drückte auf den ‹false›-Knopf. Sakina hadn't a clue. Not only did she know nothing about Irish Saints, she had never heard of a *Fiaker, fiacre* or *fiaccero*. Mentally she tossed a coin and went for the ‹true› button.

Florian konnte es kaum glauben, dass die beiden ‹true› gedrückt hatten. Wie konnten sie bloß! Zu seiner großen Überraschung erklärte Ginger Marley, dass das stimmte. Also hatte er das zusätzliche Glied vermasselt. Mist! Aber immerhin, vier Richtige in dieser Runde. Die Cyclists hatten nur zweimal Glück gehabt. Am Ende der Runde stand es 7 : 6 für die Jugglers. Uns holen die Cyclists nicht mehr so leicht ein, dachte Florian; ein wenig war er in Gedanken schon beim Halbfinale – gegen die Floppies. Das würde was werden!

«In our final round», Ginger Marley explained the rules to the television camera, «the teams once more face *questions* and tasks from the area of knowledge, skill and mixed bag. Once again they have to nominate a team member for each area – remember it has to be someone who didn't cover that area in Round 1 – and, as in the first round, they have to successfully complete three tasks in a row in order to get a link in the chain. The difference between this round and the first round is that here the teams have the opportunity to decide whether to play safe or take a risk. A risk question or task is more difficult than the others, but if three of them are achieved in a row, then the team gets two links instead of just one. The score is now 7 : 6 for the Jugglers, so they have to start.»

In dieser Runde sollte Florian für den Bereich Wissen zuständig sein, Una für Geschicklichkeit und Sakina für Potpourri. Sie beschlossen, im ersten Durchgang dieser Runde nicht auf Risiko zu gehen, sondern die normalen Aufgaben zu fordern.

An der Anzeigetafel leuchtete das Wissensgebiet für Florian auf: ‹science and inventions›. Pech aber auch! Warum konnte das blöde Licht denn nicht bei der Popmusik stehen bleiben! Wenn man eine Scheibe, die zur Hälfte rot und zur Hälfte grün ist, schnell dreht, so wurde er gefragt, was sieht man dann. Seine Antwort – rot-grüne Streifen – war falsch. Eine braune Fläche sollte es sein.

Una felt nervous about her skill task. Skill wasn't really her strong point. She was shown a bottle on a table, about two-thirds full of liquid. Afterwards she was given a picture of an identical, but empty bottle. The bottle was tilted at an angle of 30°. She was told to imagine it was the original bottle and she had to draw a line across it on the page to show where the water came up to. Easy, she thought, leaned her head to one side and drew the line.

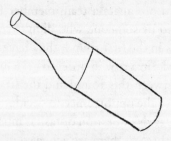

Una, nicht da, hätte Florian ihr fast zugerufen, aber das durfte er natürlich nicht.

«I'm sorry, Una», said Ginger Marley sweetly, but water isn't solid. Your picture should have looked like this.

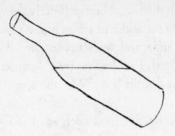

«It might interest you to know that this little test was recently given to a large group consisting of both men and women. 75 % of the men got it right, while 100 % of the women got it wrong. If it's any consolation, Una, you are not alone», Ginger Marley beamed.

Stupid cow, thought Una, of course it isn't any consolation. But she, too, smiled for the television cameras. And Lars, from the Cyclists, smiled at her. Florian sah das auch und konnte sich nicht entscheiden, ob es ein freundliches oder ein hämisches Lächeln war. Jetzt sah es natürlich viel besser für die aus. So ein Mist.

The only one of the Jugglers to do her task properly was Sakina who, seeing that they had such a bad start, decided to go for a risk question. If the other two got their next tasks right when it was their turn again, then they could make up for the lost link.

Aber erst mal waren die Cyclists dran. Das Pech der Jugglers schien sie anzuspornen. Sie entschieden sich gleich für Risiko. Barbara aus Belfast beantwortete eine schwierige Wissensfrage aus dem Unterbereich ‹Geschichte›, und Maria Angeles aus Murcia schaffte im letzten Augenblick ihre Geschicklichkeitsaufgabe. Don't let Lars be able to do his mixed bag task, prayed Una, even though she found him definitely the most interesting male candidate so far and had given him a record 8 out of 10. Still, a quiz is a quiz and we want to win, she thought. Her praying did no good. Lars had no trouble making sure that his team won its first double link. Now the score was 8 : 7 for the Cyclists.

Florian wusste, dass er jetzt auch auf Risiko gehen musste. Aber bevor es weitergehen konnte, hörte Florian Sakina sagen: «We'll be back in a minute.» Sie packte Una am Arm und beide verschwanden schnell aus der Dekoration. Florian war total verblüfft. Die andere Mannschaft wohl auch. Ginger Marley war verärgert. «Where do they think they are going?»

Outside the studio door Sakina led Una to the room where the contestants could sit when they were waiting. Una sat down while Sakina got her a glass of water. «Do you want to put your feet up?», she asked.

«No, I'll be okay in a minute. Thanks, Sakina. How did you know I was going to faint?»

«It wasn't difficult. You looked kind of grey and your eyes kept getting bigger and bigger. When you started clinging onto the stand in front of you as if your life depended on it, I thought I should do something.»

«I felt awful but I didn't know what to do. I didn't want to stop the show.»

«Do you often faint?»

«No, only at this time of the month. I'm feeling better already though. You're a real friend.»

«You'd do the same for me, I'm sure», Sakina said.

Auf eine Anordnung des Aufnahmeleiters ging Joanne hinter den beiden her. Mein Gott, sind Una und Sakina etwa auf die verrückte Idee gekommen, jetzt Rosemarys Videokassette suchen zu gehen, durchfuhr es Florian plötzlich. Dann darf Joanne sie nicht erwischen. Schnell ging er hinter Joanne her, vielleicht konnte er die beiden ja dadurch warnen, dass er sich sehr laut mit Joanne unterhielt.

«Look, I'm sorry about all this stupid business», Una said to Sakina.

«What stupid business?»

«Well, Florian.»

«What about him?»

«Well, the fact that we both, well, are sort of after him. I think I haven't been very nice to you because of it. But I've decided you can have him now, because I'm more interested in someone else», she smiled.

Sakina laughed. «Well, thanks a million. As it happens, I'm more interested in someone else, too.»

«Oh my God!» Una stood up. She had got colour back into her face now and was obviously not going to faint any more. «I hope it's not the same somebody.»

«Well, you tell me who yours is», suggested Sakina, «and then I'll tell you if it's the same one.»

Una frowned. «No. I think we should count to three and say the names at the same time. That seems fairer.»

«Okay. One, two, three…»

«Was soll das denn!» Florian und Joanne kamen in das Kandidatenzimmer gestürmt, als sich Una und Sakina gerade gleichzeitig etwas zuriefen. Dann fingen beide an zu kichern und sagten: «Thank goodness for that!»

Joanne fand das gar nicht lustig. «What are the two of you up to?»

Zu Florians Erstaunen erklärte Sakina, dass Una fast im Studio in Ohnmacht gefallen wäre und dass sie ihr geholfen habe. Donnerwetter, dachte Florian, eine schnelle Ausrede. Ob sie sich die vorher ausgedacht hatten? Aber das Gelächter hätten sie weglassen sollen. Das passte schlecht zur Ohnmacht.

Joanne sagte bloß: «You should never leave the studio again without you asking first. If Una had given me a sign or something, I could have arranged for her to go off.» Sakina nodded.

«If you are feeling alright again, which is what it looks like to me», Joanne finished, «we can go back to the studio.»

«Thirty seconds», verkündete der Aufnahmeleiter. Florians Wissensfrage stand immer noch als Nächstes an. Er war ganz konzentriert. Eine Risikofrage im Bereich *Science and inventions*. Und das, wo er in Bio, Chemie und Physik nichts drauf hatte. Wenn er sie richtig beantworten würde und Una ihre Aufgabe schaffen könnte, dann hätten sie zwei Glieder und wieder die Führung. Ginger Marley stellte die Frage: «In which decade was the escalator or moving stairs invented by Jesse W. Reno of the USA?» Um Gottes willen! Die Rolltreppe! Keine Ahnung. Scheißfrage. Aber irgendetwas musste er antworten. Er überlegte. Neulich hatte ihm Maddy aus ihrem schlauen Buch vorgelesen, dass die Londoner *tube* als erste Untergrundbahn 1890 in Betrieb genommen war. Ein Jahrzehnt ist genauso gut wie das andere, dachte er und sagte: «The 1890s.»

«Amazing, Florian! Well done! He invented it in the year 1891.»

Florian genoss die bewundernden Blicke der beiden Mädchen aus seiner Mannschaft. And Una completed her skill task successfully, too. She let out a little squeal of joy! They were in the lead again – 9 : 8.

Now Sakina had to decide whether to take a risk question or not. Again her answer could be the first of the three correct answers needed for a link. Should she go for the double or would a normal one be enough? If the Cyclists got their next ones right… She looked at Florian and Una and decided to take the risk. Sakina answered the question correctly. Now it was the Cyclist's turn again. What would they do? They went for the risk as well. Barbara answered her question on history correctly but Maria Angeles failed her skill task. They had to start saving for a link again. It was still 9 : 8 for the Jugglers. Lars chose a risk mixed bag task and managed to get it right.

Florian atmete tief durch. 9 : 8 vorne. Wenn er und Una ihre Risikoaufgaben schafften, hätten sie 11. Dann konnten sie nicht mehr überholt werden. Ein Lächeln ging über sein Gesicht. Maddy, Manni, Henk, zieht euch warm an! Wir kommen und schlagen euch im Halbfinale!

«Ready, Florian?», fragte Ginger. Florian nickte. «What is it? Before 1727 there were already fourteen British patents for it, but the first one that could actually be used was built in America in 1775 by D. Bushnell. During the First World War one was involved in the Lusitania incident.»

«Ein U-Boot, äh, u-boat», sagte Florian erleichtert.

«I'll accept that for submarine», said Ginger.

Nicht zu fassen, freute sich Florian. Noch vor drei Tagen hätte er keine Chance gehabt, diese Frage zu beantworten. Was interessierte ihn, wofür die Briten vor Ewigkeiten vierzehn Patente erhalten hatten. Aber im MOMI hatten sie im blöden *World War One*-Room einen Wochenschauausschnitt gesehen, in dem der Untergang der Lusitania gezeigt wurde. Da habe ich aber Glück gehabt, dachte er. Nun blieb nur noch Unas Aufgabe.

Una listened while her task was explained. She was brought over to a wire fence which was a little taller than she was. Her ‹risk› task was to stand in front of it and try to manœuvre a tennis ball, which was behind it, up over the fence. She fiddled around for a while before she discovered the best way to do it, then slowly, sticking her fingers through the holes in the wire, she passed the ball up from the fingers of one hand to those of the other. She started to sweat. «Come on, Una, you're doing fine», she heard Sakina say when she was about half way there. She was concentrating hard and even forgot the cameras for a moment. Slowly, slowly the ball crept upwards. Two-thirds, three-quarters of the way. Nearly there. One last careful little push with the fingers of her left hand and the ball would be at the top. Concentrate, Una, concentrate. Bong. Oh no. The time was up.

No link in the chain for the Jugglers. After all that hard work! She was very disappointed. When she saw the disappointment on the face of Florian and Sakina, too, she tried to cheer them up by saying: «Maybe the Cyclists won't get theirs right either and we'll still win.»

Aber die Cyclists machten keine Fehler mehr und gewannen das Spiel. 10:9 lautete der Endstand. «What an exciting game!», rief Ginger Marley, «so close! First class television as I am sure our audience at home in front of their screens will agree. Well done to the Cyclists who now go on into the semifinal where they will play against Floppies. Our commiserations to the Jugglers. You played a great game but, as they say, the best team won!»

Shut up, you stupid cow, thought Una. As soon as the credits rolled, she rushed away from the set.

«She's upset, let her go», Sakina said to Florian as he started

132

to go after Una, «she probably thinks it's her fault that we didn't win.»

Sie mussten lange warten, bis Joanne sie nach Hause fahren konnte. Ein blödes Herumhängen war das, weil sie dabei zusehen mussten, wie jeder den Cyclists gratulierte. Als Una endlich wieder auftauchte, hatte sie sich ein wenig gefasst und sah nicht mehr so deprimiert aus.

«I'm really sorry», said Maddy when she heard that they had lost.

«Wieso? Du hast doch immer gesagt, wir schaffen es nicht», knurrte Florian.

«That was just talk», Maddy replied. «I'm sorry. I was hoping we could beat *you* in the semifinal.» Florian bombardierte sie mit einem Sofakissen.

Maddy grinned. «But we'll punish the Cyclists for what they did to you, okay?»

«Okay», antworteten Florian und Sakina.

Una had been sitting there quietly saying nothing. «You are very quiet, Una. I hope you aren't thinking about your last task», Sakina tried to comfort her.

A big smile broke out on Una's face. «Thinking about my last task only cheers me up. I did very well indeed», she said and pulled a video tape out of her bag.

«Una, you didn't!», shrieked Sakina.

«Una, you are wonderful», rief Florian und fiel ihr förmlich um den Hals.

«Would someone like to tell me what's going on?», Maddy asked.

Chapter thirteen

****

in which Sakina and Manni are given two explanations
und in dem Florian und Una ein Loch
in einer Biographie feststellen

Maddy had spent the day at home reading her book on general knowledge. Manni und Henk waren einen halben Tag lang im Museum of the Moving Image herumspaziert. Einfach nur so. Was Florian und Sakina darüber berichtet hatten, klang so toll, dass man da auch hingehen konnte, ohne einen falschen Andy zu beschatten. In der Buchhandlung des Museums hatten sie dann im *Who's Who in the Media in Britain* unter Stephen Robinson nachgeschlagen. Er war «one of the biggest independent producers» stand dort. Das wussten sie schon. Aber der Satz «he graduated from Oxford in 1964» war interessant.

Nach der Besichtigung des MOMI wollten sie in das Hotel zurück, in dem sie und die anderen Kandidaten untergebracht waren. Vielleicht konnte man von denen was erfahren. Aber was? Dazu kam es nicht, denn sie waren kaum im Hotel angekommen, als Una anrief und von der Videokassette erzählte. Da mussten sie natürlich sofort zu den Butlers fahren.

For somebody who had just messed up the last question, losing her team the game, Una was in remarkably good form. She told them how she had managed to slip into the office while everyone was still in the studio, had found Rosemary's bag and taken the tape that was in it.

«How can you be sure that it is the right one?», meldete Manni Zweifel an.

«I can't, but we'll soon know for sure», Una replied. She pressed the play button.

SUPERCHAIN

The Super European Quiz Show.
Rehearsal 1.
Hostess: Rosemary Baker

---

lasen sie in dem Vorspann.

«Klasse!», «that's it!», «the proof!», «jetzt haben wir endlich einen Beweis», redeten sie alle durcheinander, als klar wurde, dass sie tatsächlich die Probe für die Folge mit dem ersten Andy erwischt hatten.

«Okay, we have real proof now of what we knew already», said Maddy after the initial excitement had cooled down, «but where does that lead us?»

Tja, dachte Florian. Eigentlich waren sie keinen Schritt weiter. Immer noch wussten sie nicht, warum die Andys ausgetauscht worden waren. Nur dass sie es waren, das konnten sie jetzt beweisen.

«Well, nowhere really», Sakina answered Maddy's question, «but we should keep trying. The three of you are in the studio tomorrow. Maybe one of us should go there to be in the audience and see whether we can't find something out.»

Florian konnte sich nicht so recht vorstellen, was man im

Studio noch herausfinden konnte; außerdem hatte er nach der Niederlage auch keine Lust mehr, dort aufzukreuzen. Una didn't seem to feel like it either.

«Okay, I'll go», said Sakina. She looked at Florian and Una. «Maybe the two of you could go to Wapping.»

Wapping – das klang nach einem Riesen-Hamburger. Florian war irritiert. Außerdem – wieso warf Sakina Una so einen komischen Blick zu? Seit heute Nachmittag waren die beiden etwas komisch. Auf dem Rückweg vom Studio hatte er nur gesagt, dass die Ausrede mit der Ohnmacht ganz toll gewesen war, aber nicht mit ihrem Gelächter zusammengepasst hatte. Die beiden hatten ihn einen Augenblick angesehen und waren dann in ein minutenlanges hysterisches Lachen ausgebrochen. Weiber!

«Wapping is where the head office of Andy's father's media company is», Maddy explained to him, «remember what Henk and Sakina found out? Maybe the two of you can just hang around there and see what happens.»

«Maybe», sagte Florian und dachte, vor einem großen Zeitungshaus rumzuhängen bringt sicher noch weniger, als sich im Studio als Zuschauer zu langweilen. Er schaute Una an. Die gab ihm einen aufmunternden Blick: «Shall we?»

Warum nicht?

«All right, girls and boys, it's time for a break», Rosemary ended the rehearsal. Sakina was the only person sitting in the audience. The ‹real› audience would only be let in after the end of the rehearsal. She wanted to see the show from the other side and to see the Cyclists being beaten, she had said and Joanne didn't have any objections.

«Sollen wir in die Kantine gehen?», fragte Manni, der zu ihr rüberkam. Sakina nodded. Maddy and even Henk were busy talking to people from the production team.

«Any idea what we are supposed to do?», Una asked Florian when they were walking out of the Wapping underground station.

Florian zuckte mit den Schultern. Irgendwas über Andys Vater herausfinden, irgendwas, das einem weiterhalf. Weiterhalf? Wohin? Wozu?

«Never mind», Una said, «either we'll find whatever it is we are looking for or else we'll have a great day anyway.»

«Yes», antwortete Florian. *A great day* war auf jeden Fall gut; vielleicht mussten sie ja auch Pärchen spielen, um etwas herauszubekommen, wie Maddy und Manni vor drei Tagen. Bei dem Gedanken wurde ihm ganz warm.

They walked to the head office and hung around there for about ten minutes, keeping an eye on the building. «This is stupid», said Una finally, «we could stand here all day and still nothing will happen.» Florian gab ihr Recht. Aber was sonst konnten sie machen?

Auf dem Weg in die Kantine begegneten Manni und Sakina Derek.

«Hi», sagte er. «Have you got a minute, Sakina? I'd like to have a word with you.»

Sakina raised her eyebrows. «Can Manni come, too?», she asked.

Derek frowned. «I suppose so. He probably knows about it as well. The Floppies and the Jugglers do a lot together, don't they?» Sie folgten ihm ins Büro.

«Remember you asked me a while ago whether I noticed anything peculiar about Andy from the Argonauts?», Derek asked Sakina.

She couldn't believe her ears. Why was he asking her that now? She nodded.

«Well, I can tell you now what happened. You were right when you noticed that the Andy you saw on the television wasn't the one you had seen in the studio. It was a different Andy.»

Warum erzählt er uns das jetzt, fragte sich Manni, und – vor allen Dingen – was wird er erzählen? Er hörte gespannt zu.

«You see, after the first episode with the original Andy – Andy Korbel – was recorded he got very sick and had to go to hospital. His doctor said that he would be there for at least a month.»

So so, dachte Manni. Die haben wohl von Sakina und Andy Hedley im MOMI erfahren und wollen uns jetzt eine Erklärung geben.

«Poor Andy», said Sakina sounding honestly sorry, «what is wrong with him?»

«Something with his kidneys, I think», Derek continued. «Now as you know all the remaining episodes of SUPER-CHAIN are being recorded now and will be finished by the time he comes out of hospital. But the episode of you against the Argonauts had already been recorded before it happened and they had to decide what to do.»

«They?», Sakina interrupted.

«Production. Anyway they decided that it would be stupid to look for a brand new team to replace the Argonauts and to start all over again. The fairest thing seemed to be to replace Andy Korbel – by a friend of his, Andy Hedley – and to have

Andy Hedley give the same answers on a new recording as Andy Korbel had done on the old one. So that's what they did.»

«Why didn't you tell us this before now?», Sakina asked.

Gute Frage, dachte Manni, darauf fällt ihm bestimmt keine gute Antwort ein. Interessant, dass sie eine Krankenhaus-Ausrede gewählt hatten. Also hatte Andy Korbel seinem Vater nichts von dem Treffen im Park erzählt. Sehr gut. Irgendwie war er wohl doch auf ihrer Seite.

«That's difficult to answer», Derek replied after pausing for a moment, «for some reason they wanted to keep it hush-hush – it might damage the reputation of the company. You do understand of course that I am telling you this in confidence. In strictest confidence. But when they realized that you had noticed it, and you are the only team who ever saw Andy Korbel, they thought that maybe you should be told.»

«That's thoughtful of them», Sakina said, «we had been wondering about it. But it's all clear to me now. Just one more question – if Andy Korbel is still in hospital, maybe we could send him a card or something.»

«He is still in hospital, but I don't know where», said Derek.

Manni sah ihn genau an. Er wirkte nicht so, als ob er log – oder war er nur ein sehr guter Lügner? –, er wirkte, als ob er die Geschichte selber glaubte. «How did they replace him on the recording?», fragte Manni.

Derek schaute ihn leicht irritiert an. «The story of how they replaced him is complicated. You'd have to ask someone from VT how that works.»

«And what happens if we tell someone about this exchange of candidates?», fragte Manni weiter.

«That wouldn't be in your own interest», said Derek seriously. «If the press hears about it, we will have to cancel the whole show. And SUPERCHAIN is just a game after all. We think what we did is fair, but others might think it's a bit unorthodox.»

Ein bisschen unorthodox ist gut, dachte Manni. Voll gelogen ist es. Aber wenn er Andy nicht vor drei Tagen selbst gesehen hätte, hätte er Dereks Geschichte echt geglaubt. So überzeugend war sie.

«What do we know about Gary Korbel so far?», asked Una after they had been in Wapping for a while. «He studied at Oxford. He finished there in 1964. From the end of the 1970s onwards he made a lot of money in the media in Australia. He now owns a quality newspaper as well as TV and film studios. That was what was on Henk's photocopy.»

Florian überlegte einen Moment. «It didn't really say what he did between 1964 and the late 70s, did it?», sagte er dann.

«No», Una confirmed, «just that he worked for the newspaper which he now owns.»

Das bringt uns alles nicht weiter, dachte Florian. Henk und Sakina hatten was rausgefunden, warum fiel ihm und Una denn nichts ein?

«Shall we just call it a day», suggested Una, «and have a mooch in a record shop or two?»

Florian nickte. Geschlagen machten sie sich auf den Weg zurück zur U-Bahn.

Sakina was sitting alone in the first row of the audience, watching the show. The Floppies were doing really well. Sakina noticed how nervous she became when they paused over a question, but they were in the lead after Round 3. During the short break before the final round Manni walked over to Sakina.

«Have you told Maddy and Henk what Derek told us?», she asked him.

«Yeah…» Sein Blick fiel auf Ginger Marley, die zu ihnen herüberkam. Sakina noticed her as well. She quickly changed languages: «Vielleicht sagt sie uns auch was über A…», better not use the name right now, she thought, «unseren Freund und das Krankenhaus.»

«Hello, Sakina», said Ginger Marley, «nice to see you here again. Enjoying yourself?» Sie gab Manni ein kurzes professionelles Lächeln.

«Oh yes, thank you», said Sakina. So Ginger Marley recognized her and remembered her name without the help of a cuecard. «Has Derek spoken to you today?», she asked.

«Yes, he has.»

«About Andy?», Ginger continued.

Aha, dachte Manni. Das ist es also. Sie will nochmal die Krankenhausgeschichte loswerden. Doppelt hält besser. ‹Die› müssen ja ziemlich nervös geworden sein.

Sakina replied: «Yes, Derek told us all about it. I was wondering whether we could visit him in hospital. Do you know where he is?»

Ginger Marley frowned. «Well, that's what I wanted to speak to you about.» Sie sah sich um, aber außer Manni und Sakina war niemand in Hörweite. Wieder gab sie Manni ein gewinnendes Lächeln und wandte sich dann an Sakina. «You see, Andy isn't in hospital at all.»

Sakina stared at her. What the hell is going on, she thought.

Was ist das denn, dachte Manni. Wieso kommen die denn jetzt mit zwei Geschichten? Wussten sie doch von Una und

Andy Korbel im Park? Wollte sie bloß einen Denkfehler von Derek korrigieren?

«Now look, Sakina, you are obviously an intelligent girl», Ginger Marley went on, «and you realized very early that something funny was going on. I think you should know the whole story. You see, when Andy Korbel applied with his teammates to take part in ‹Superchain› and was accepted by us, there was one very important factor which we had failed to notice. Andy's father owns the production company which makes the show. Now Andy is a bright boy and his team would have good chances of winning. You can imagine how the press would react if they found out that one of the winners of a television quiz was the son of the owner of the company who made the quiz, can't you?»

Sakina nodded her head. Yes she could.

Manni hielt den Atem an. Das war es also! Dem Alten gehörte die Sendung, und er wollte nicht, dass sein Sohn sie gewann. Eigentlich verständlich. Oder war das nur eine neue Geschichte? Ginger war inzwischen fortgefahren: «It was our fault in production. We should have spotted his name straight away – it's not as if it is a difficult one to spot – and told him he couldn't participate. Luckily we realized our mistake after the first episode with his team, so we were able to repair it to some degree», Ginger Marley paused.

«Why did Derek tell me Andy was in hospital, then?», Sakina wanted to know.

«Well, Sakina, as I'm sure you can understand this whole affair is extremely embarrassing for us. It was a major mistake on our part. So we have told anyone who needed an explanation that Andy had to go to hospital. And we told everybody up till today not to say anything to your team about it because we thought you wouldn't notice. We didn't know how clever you were. And your team as well of course», wandte sie sich Manni zu. «You would make a great detective the way you pretended to be so interested in TV production yesterday, you know.»

Das ging Manni runter wie Butter. Trotzdem stimmte da irgendwas noch nicht, warnte ihn eine dünne Stimme im Hinterkopf. Aber was?

Ginger looked at them seriously. «Judging by the questions you are asking, you and your friends are obviously concerned about Andy. You can tell the others on your teams what I have told you, but I hope you realize that it is in the strictest confidence.»

«Yes, Ginger», said Sakina. Manni nickte.

Vierzehntes Kapitel

****

*in dem Florian und Una ganz europäisch werden
and in which Henk is a walking calculator*

«Would it help if we knew where Gary Korbel was between 1964 and the late 1970s?», asked Una while they were waiting for the tube to arrive. Florian nickte. Vielleicht – vielleicht auch nicht, dachte er.

«But we can't just walk into his office and ask», sagte er, «he probably gave that part of the information about himself…» – was zum Teufel hieß ‹absichtlich› und was hieß ‹vage›? – «he probably gave it purposely non-exact.»

Una looked puzzled. «Absichtlich vage», sagte er ungeduldig, obwohl er wusste, dass das Una nichts nützen würde.

«*Vage*? Oh – vague», she understood what he meant. «Yes, yes. He probably left it vague on purpose.»

Florian kam eine Idee. Eine der Sachen, die ihn im Deutschunterricht im letzten Jahr am meisten genervt hatten, war ein Projekt gewesen, bei dem sie sich über die Veränderungen von Zeitungen nach dem Krieg hatten informieren sollen. Stundenlang hatten sie in einem Archiv alte, übel riechende, verstaubte Zeitungen durchblättern müssen. Echt ätzend war das gewesen. Nur Silvia war voll drauf abgefahren. Aber die machte ja auch die Schülerzeitung und wollte Journalistin werden. Vielleicht brauchte sie auch einfach ein paar Schleimpunkte für ihre Deutschnote. Aber wenn sie jetzt so tun würden, als ob sie ein Projekt machten? Die Zeitung hatte sicher ein Archiv.

Una noticed how Florian's face lit up. When he started to explain about a school project she didn't understand what he was on about but then it dawned on her. Of course! If they looked through the newspapers that Andy's father was working on from 1964 onwards, they might at least find out where he had been at that time or even what he was doing.

«Do you think we'll find anything?», asked Florian, «it's a lot of newspaper. And would they let us in? What kind of story can we tell them?»

Sie überlegten eine Weile hin und her.

Then Una said: «Remember when we looked at Henk's photocopy, Manni got all excited and said that the journalism bit was probably just... what did he call ‹camouflage› – oh yes, *Toy-shunk* – and that Andy's father could have been a spy or drug-dealer and that's how he got rich.»

Florian musste lachen. So wie Una ‹Täuschung› aussprach, klang es eher wie ein englisch-chinesisches Spielzeug. «But never mind the spy or drug-dealer part», she continued, «the fact that he was abroad is the important bit. He didn't want Andy to be in the quiz because it would be shown on European TV. So he must be afraid of...» She couldn't think what he could be afraid of.

Sie hat Recht, dachte Florian, irgendwas ist irgendwo auf dem Kontinent passiert, und er will nicht, dass man ihn durch seinen Sohn dort erkennt. Er war Journalist und er war auf dem Kontinent. Vielleicht war er Auslandskorrespondent. Aber wo?

Una agreed with Florian when he told her his speculation. «So we need to pretend we are doing a project which has something to do with international news», she said.

Florian nickte. Er fand Projekte wegen der Arbeit, die mit

ihnen verbunden war, schon schlimm genug. Und nun sollte er sich sogar eins ausdenken. Uaagh.

«I've got it!», Una declared and pulled Florian by the arm.

«Ready Henk?», asked Ginger Marley. «If you answer this mixed bag risk question your team will get two links, bringing the score up to 11 for the Floppies.»

Manni biss sich auf die Lippe. Es war die letzte Runde. Die Cyclists hatten bisher acht Glieder der Kette. Und nur noch eine Chance, höchstens zwei weitere zu bekommen. Das hieß, wenn Henk die Frage richtig beantworten würde, wären die Floppies im Finale. Manni hielt die Spannung kaum noch aus.

«I'm ready», said Henk.

«It's a mental arithmetic question. You have to follow the instructions I'll give you using three digits for every stage. Remember, zero counts as a digit as well. You have 45 seconds. The time starts after I have finished the instructions. So please concentrate: Pick any number consisting of three different digits. Reverse the order of this number and subtract the smaller of your two numbers from the larger. Take the result and reverse the digits of it. Then add this result to the number you have just reversed. Your time starts now.»

Henk stand regungslos mit geschlossenen Augen da. Die Uhr tickte. Alle hielten den Atem an. Manni fragte sich, wie Ginger Marley überhaupt wissen konnte, ob die Antwort, die Henk geben würde, richtig war. Gut, dass er diese Aufgabe nicht erwischt hatte. Aber vielleicht hatte Henk eine Chance.

«One thousand and eighty-nine», said Henk.

«Congratulations Henk, well done», Ginger Marley beamed. She looked into the camera. «If any of you at home tried to do that task you should have ended up with the same answer. It is one of the miracles of mathematics that this formula produces the answer 1089 no matter what three different digits are taken at the beginning.»

Unglaublich, dachte Manni. Und probierte es aus. Ganz langsam: eine dreistellige Zahl: 321. Umgekehrte Reihenfolge der Ziffern: 123. Die kleinere von der größeren abziehen. Das dauerte einige Zeit. Kopfrechnen war wirklich nicht seine Sache. Für so was gab es normalerweise schließlich Taschenrechner! 321 weniger 123. 198. Und jetzt? Dieses Ergebnis umdrehen: 891. 891 und 198, das war... tatsächlich, das war 1089. Ein toller Trick. Den merk ich mir, dachte er.

Spitze. Absolute Spitze. Während Florian eine Zeitung nach der anderen vom großen Stapel nahm und sie Seite für Seite durchblätterte, waren seine Gedanken immer noch voller Bewunderung bei Una. Mit welcher Frechheit und Selbstsicherheit sie aufgetreten war. «Excuse me», hatte sie beim Portier angefangen, «my Dublin school and Florian's school in Berlin are doing an exchange. Financed by Brussels, you know.» Und dann hatte sie erzählt, dass Teil des Austauschs ein Projekt war, bei dem man herausfinden sollte, was über Irland in deutschen und über Berlin in irischen Tageszeitungen berichtet worden war. «And here we are in London now on a one day stopover between exchanges», hatte sie voller Begeisterung gesagt, «and we thought it would be especially good if we could find out how an English paper wrote about the two places during the same period.» Sie hatte noch was von guten Noten, die sie dafür kriegen würden, gesagt und sich entschuldigt, dass sie so unangemeldet kommen würden, aber sie hätten gerade erst die Idee gehabt. Florian wusste nicht, ob es an Unas unwiderstehlicher Art lag oder daran, dass der Portier aus Irland stammte, jedenfalls waren sie bis zum Archivar vorgedrungen. Und auch der hatte Unas eindringliche Schilderung geglaubt.

Florian blätterte und blätterte. Una turned page after page. 1965 nothing, 1966 nothing, 1967 nothing. Una sighed. Would they ever find anything? Maybe they should have gone to the record shops after all.

Da – fast hätte Florian geschrien, wenn er sich nicht gerade noch erinnert hätte, dass ihr Projekt sicher keinen Freudenschrei erlaubte. Er stieß Una an: «That looks like an interesting article about Berlin», sagte er möglichst gleichgültig und zeigte auf eine Reportage über ‹Students unrest in Berlin›. Una stared at it. There it was. ‹From our Berlin correspondent, Gary Korbel›.

«Henk, you are wonderful», Maddy gave him a big hug and a kiss as soon as the recording was over. «Echt irre», klopfte ihm Manni auf die Schulter. «Congratulations again», kam Ginger Marley zu ihnen herüber, «you are a great team.»

Manni sah ihr fest in die Augen. Sie war die Freundlichkeit in Person, wirkte ruhig und ehrlich. Hatte sie ihm und Sakina vorhin endlich die Wahrheit gesagt?

«So, I'll see you in the final the day after tomorrow. You'll be playing against either the Fanclub or the Argonauts.»

Ein kaum merkbares Augenzwinkern, so kam es Manni vor, begleitete die Erwähnung der ‹Argonauts›.

«Could I have tickets for four people to come to see the final, please?», Maddy asked. «I think my mother might like to come and the Jugglers definitely want to be there – especially if we are going to play against the Argonauts.»

«Sure», Ginger answered, «I'll arrange for Joanne to get them for you.»

As soon as Ginger left, Sakina went over to her three friends and she and Manni told Henk and Maddy what Ginger had said to them during the break.

«So that's it», said Maddy, «it sounds plausible, doesn't it?» She looked a little disappointed. «Just a simple mix-up because they weren't careful enough when they chose the candidates. Well, we've certainly wasted enough time on it, haven't we?»

Manni musste lachen. Maddy war ja echt enttäuscht, dass sie jetzt keinen richtigen Fall hatten, den man aufklären konnte. Mehr um sie zu trösten, sagte er, dass er so ein komisches Gefühl habe, dass da etwas nicht stimmte.

«Bah», she exclaimed, «the Germans always doubt everything. That's why they have produced all those philosophers. At least, that's what my Grandad in Edinburgh always says.»

Manni wusste nicht, was er darauf antworten sollte. So allgemein wollte er die Sache nun auch nicht betrachten. «Well, maybe the Dutch are good philosophers too then», mischte sich Henk zu Mannis Überraschung ein. «Because I think something *is* still wrong, too.»

Alle Augen richteten sich auf Henk. «Remember that Andy Korbel said his father only behaved strangely when he heard that the show was shown outside England as well? He didn't object to it in principle. That doesn't go with Ginger's version of the story.»

«Yes», Sakina joined in, «and he wouldn't have kept saying ‹trust me, trust me› to Andy instead of giving him an explanation – he could have just told him about the production hiccup, couldn't he?»

Maddy's face lit up. Maybe there still was a case after all.

Fieberhaft blätterten Florian und Una weiter. Fanden immer mehr Artikel des Berlin-Korrespondenten Gary Korbel. Dann plötzlich keinen mehr. Hatten sie etwas übersehen? Florian ging einige Monate zurück. Sein Auge fiel auf einen Artikel: ‹Papua New Guinea gains complete independence. From our Australian correspondent, Gary Korbel›. Florian und Una sahen sich an. Von Berlin nach Australien. Ob das normal war für Auslandskorrespondenten?

«I'm afraid you'll have to go now», unterbrach eine Stimme ihre Überlegungen, «you have been here for a couple of hours and I can't let you stay any longer.» Das war der freundliche Archivar. «It wasn't strictly speaking according to the rules that I let you in here, you understand.»

«Oh, we understand», Una smiled at him, «thank you. Anyway, I think we have collected enough material now.»

She showed him a notebook filled with notes.

Die hat ja wirklich an alles gedacht, bewunderte sie Florian.

«It was very helpful», Una continued, «we have found lots of interesting material», she looked at Florian, «haven't we?»

«Ja, yes», stammelte der und drehte seinen Block um. Auf dem standen nämlich nur die Wörter Berlin und Australien und einige Jahreszahlen.

«Goodbye Mr O'Leary and thanks again», Una called to the porter as they left the building.

«Goodbye Una, and good luck with your project», he called back.

«You are wonderful», sagte Florian, als sie das Gebäude verlassen hatten. «I know», she replied and looked at him through her long black eyelashes.

«I mean... the way you talked us into the archive. That was wonderful», sagte Florian schnell.

«Oh that?» Klang sie enttäuscht? «That was nothing. You should hear my mother!»

Als alle wieder bei den Butlers eingetroffen waren, setzte das große Erzählen an. «They must be really nervous about the question we were asking. They have obviously realized that we knew about the swop otherwise they wouldn't have said anything to us», Sakina said after she had told her story.

«They don't know how much we know. But they must think that if they admit there was a swop of Andys and if they give us a reason for it, then we will stop asking uncomfortable questions», Maddy summed up the situation.

«Shit!», cursed Una. «If they are openly admitting there was a swop then our wonderful videotape isn't worth much any more, is it?»

Betretenes Schweigen. Daran hatte noch keiner gedacht.

«Who knows», versuchte es schließlich Manni, «maybe we can use it to find out more – but how?»

«We could try to beat the father at his own game», Maddy suggested, «and do something with media.»

Es dauerte fast zwei Stunden, bis sie sich Stück für Stück an einen Plan herangetastet hatten. Aus der Idee, irgendetwas mit den Medien zu machen, hatte sich schließlich die Idee entwickelt, Gary Korbel durch, wie Maddy sagte, einen ‹home-made media overkill› zu verwirren und ihn so vielleicht dazu zu bringen, etwas zu verraten. Der Plan beruhte auf unbewiesenen Annahmen und hatte noch viele Löcher, aber immerhin – es war ein Plan.

Am nächsten Tag, am Sonntag, fanden keine Aufnahmen statt. Die sechs trafen sich bei den Butlers, um gemeinsam SUPER-CHAIN im Fernsehen zu sehen. Es handelte sich um das zweite Ausscheidungsspiel, das die Cyclists haushoch gewannen. «Imagine», Sakina said, «that's still the Qualifying

Round. In the meantime they have beaten us and the Floppies have beaten them in the semifinal.» Danach machten sie sich an die Vorbereitungen für den ‹media-overkill› für den nächsten Tag.

Maddy asked her surprised father for the number of the fax machine in his office and then went to the attic to find things which could be used to make her look like a courier.

Manni setzte sich an Maddys Computer und entwarf ein auffälliges Firmenzeichen für einen Briefumschlag der Firma ‹Berlin Enterprises›.

Sakina and Henk sat down and wrote the letter which would be put into the envelope as well as two other short texts.

Florian telefonierte mit Silvia in Berlin. Es dauerte endlos, bis er sie davon überzeugen konnte, dass sie den nächsten Tag dort in einem Zeitungsarchiv verbringen sollte.

Una used all her skill to put large letters on the banner and the T-shirt which she and Florian would use the following day, and she stuck the letters for ‹Gamma Couriers› on the old leather jacket which Maddy had found in the attic.

Manni und Maddy liefen im Zimmer auf und ab, als sie die Texte, die Henk und Sakina geschrieben hatten, auswendig lernten.

Sakina felt the need, all of a sudden, to rehearse putting a tape into a video recorder although she had done it hundreds of times before.

Henk studied the map of the museum to find the quickest way for him to take.

Florian kam sich ziemlich blöd vor, als er übte, sich langsam auf der Stelle umzudrehen.

When they had everything ready they were quite tired. Mrs Butler came into the room.

«It's getting late, children», she said, «are any of you in the studio tomorrow?»

«No Mum», said Maddy, «tomorrow is our day off.»

Mrs Butler smiled. «That's good, you have a nice relaxing day ahead of you, then.»

Chapter fifteen

****

in which a media show occurs
und in dem jemand ganz schön ins Schwitzen kommt

Wearing her jacket with ‹Gamma Couriers› stuck on the back and a professional cyclist's reflective belt, Maddy arrived at the head office of Gary Korbel's newspaper the next morning. She locked her bicycle to the lamppost outside and sprinted up the steps. In one hand she was carrying a white envelope marked ‹Urgent, Confidential, Personal Delivery› and addressed to Mr Gary Korbel. It bore the sender's logo: ‹Berlin Enterprises›. In the other hand she had a clipboard with her different ‹courier› destinations written on it. She knocked at the glass window of the porter's office. «Will you take a letter for…», she looked at the envelope, «…Mr. Gary Korbel?», she asked.

«Sure», he said, «give me your clipboard and I'll sign for it.»

A minute later she was cycling off again.

«Alles klar?», fragte Florian, als Maddy zurückkam.

Maddy nodded. «Will he buy it, though?», she wondered.

«Was soll er denn kaufen?» Florian war verwirrt.

«Nothing. I meant – will he believe us?»

«Aha, ob er uns das abnimmt.»

«Why should he want to lose weight?»

Manni sah die beiden an und schüttelte den Kopf. Am Abend zuvor hatten sie endlos diskutiert, was in dem Brief an Gary Korbel stehen musste. Immer wieder hatten sie den Text geändert, bis es zum Schluss hieß:

Mr. Korbel,
Berlin Enterprises would like to meet you to
discuss a documentary for German television
about certain events which took place in Berlin in 1975. Please meet us at 3 p. m. in the TV
technology room of the Museum of the Moving
Image.

Ein Schuss ins Dunkle war das, hatte Manni gesagt, aber immerhin. Vielleicht war damals etwas in Berlin passiert, das dazu
führte, dass Andy Korbel auch heute noch nicht im europäi-
schen Fernsehen gezeigt werden durfte. Wenn das stimmte,
dann waren ‹Berlin›, ‹1975› und ‹Fernsehen› Wörter, die Andys Vater neugierig machen müssten. Und wenn nicht, dann
hatten sie nichts verloren – außer das Eintrittsgeld für das Museum.

Henk stared at the picture that Maddy had taken four days
ago. Would he recognize Gary Korbel? Anxiously he exam-
ined all the middle-aged men coming into the Museum of the
Moving Image. It wasn't that one... no, not him either... nor
that one... There! There could be no doubt about it. As soon as
he saw him walking up the stairs towards the entrance of the
museum, Henk ran. He flew through the room with early opti-
cal experiments and magic lanterns. He raced around a corner,
nearly knocking a woman over. «Sorry», he shouted and heard
her muttering a complaint as he rushed into the next room. Up
the stairs through the silent cinema section he sprinted. He
reached the TV technology room totally out of breath. He gave
the sign for ‹he's on his way!› to his friends, each of whom was
waiting at their post. The plan could go into action.

Florian atmete tief durch. Noch 120 Sekunden. In ihrem
Plan hatten sie unterstellt, dass Henk durch sein Rennen unge-

fähr zwei Minuten vor Gary Korbel im TV-Technology-Raum eintreffen würde. Hoffentlich stimmte es wirklich, dachte Florian, sonst verpufft die ganze Aktion. Noch 90 Sekunden. Er stand vor der sogenannten *stop-action*-Kamera. Sie nahm Museumsbesucher auf und zeigte sie ungefähr eine Minute später in ruckhaften Bildfolgen. Noch 60 Sekunden. Florian trat vor die Kamera, stand einige Sekunden still und drehte sich dann langsam wie ein Roboter, bis er mit dem Rücken zur Kamera stand. Dann drehte er sich wieder nach vorne. Diese Sequenz wiederholte er mehrmals. Ob die Buchstaben auf dem T-Shirt groß genug waren?

60 seconds to go. Una got into position to fly over the Thames. She lay on her stomach on the blue ramp, turned to the right and to the left, rolled over on her back and then onto her stomach again to face the water in the film. All this time the ‹Superman› music was blaring in her ears. She was enjoying every minute of it. When she reached the Tower of London, she looked at her watch. It was nearly time. Just ten seconds to go before she had to pull the banner out of her pocket.

Noch 60 Sekunden. Manni saß aufgeregt in der Interview-Kabine. Gut, dass es heute relativ leer war und er ohne Schwierigkeiten um drei Uhr an die Reihe kam. Seine echten Antworten auf die gefilmten Fragen des Interviewers wurden aufgenommen. Manni fing an, über einen deutschen Film zu berichten. Das Interessante an diesem Film war, dass die Hauptrolle von einem jungen Engländer gespielt wurde, der als Teilnehmer in einem internationalen Quiz im Fernsehen aufgetreten war.

60 seconds. «And now I'll hand you over to our correspondent at the Museum of the Moving Image on the South Bank», said the newscaster from News at Ten. Maddy looked straight

into the camera and gave her report. If everything worked out all right it should appear on the screen in the TV technology room just as Gary Korbel was entering. So would Manni's interview and Florian's jerky movements. Would their timing be right?

Manni starrte zum Eingang. Sein Interview war fertig. Kein Gary Korbel. Der Vorspann zu seinem Interview und der zu Maddys Nachrichtensendung liefen auf den Bildschirmen, Una flog über die Themse, Florian zuckte über seinen Bildschirm – wo blieb Korbel? Hatte Henk den falschen Mann identifiziert?

Da – endlich! Manni beobachtete ihn genau. Gary Korbel kam in den Raum, sah sich um und blieb plötzlich wie hypnotisiert stehen, sein Gesicht wurde ganz weiß. Von allen Seiten drang es auf ihn ein. Ein Mädchen flog als Superman durch die Gegend – an ihrer Hand flatterte ein Banner – WATCH ANDY KORBEL ON SUPERCHAIN stand darauf in großen Buchstaben. Auf einem Bildschirm interviewte ein bekannter Filmkritiker einen Jungen, der sagte «and so he was spotted in a TV quiz. But I think, with this film, Andy Korbel is soon going to be a big name in Germany.» Auf einem anderen Bildschirm sah er in sprunghaften Bildern einen Jungen sich umdrehen: WHERE IS, stand auf der Vorderseite seines T-Shirts, ANDY KORBEL auf der Rückseite. Manni sah, wie die Augen des Gary Korbel unruhig von Bildschirm zu Bildschirm wanderten, jetzt starrten sie auf die Nachrichtensendung, in der Maddy verkündete: «There is great excitement here at the MOMI today, with rumors claiming that a candidate from a well known quiz programme has simply been removed from the recording of the episode in which he appeared. A speaker for the production company denies all reports of the removal, but other candidates who were involved say that it is true and unconfirmed reports hint that they can prove it. The question on everybody's mind at present is: why should anyone go to such length to remove a candidate from the programme? There will be a special showing of the quiz in question in the home video section of this room now.»

Manni sah die Schweißperlen auf Gary Korbels Stirn glänzen. Wie von einem Magneten angezogen, ging er in die hintere Ecke des Raums, wo über einer Sitzgruppe das Schild ‹SHOW YOUR OWN HOME VIDEO› hing. Schritt für Schritt gingen Maddy, Manni, Una und Florian hinter ihm her. Henk stayed in the background. He was what Florian had called ‹Beschattungsreserve›. It meant that he would follow Korbel if he left before they had found out what they wanted.

Sakina stood at the video recorder which was for the use of visitors of the MOMI. There they could show their own videos. When Gary Korbel started walking towards her she pressed the ‹play› button. The titles rolled:

SUPERCHAIN

The Super European Quiz Show.
Rehearsal 1.
Hostess: Rosemary Baker

When the tape got to the part where Andy and the other Argonauts were in view, she pressed the ‹pause› button.

Manni starrte auf Gary Korbel. Der drehte sich um und sah

alle der Reihe nach an. Nur Maddy hielt seinem Blick stand. «Very smart, very smart indeed. What a fine media show you have put on for my benefit», Gary Korbel tried to sound calm but he looked shaken. «Who put you up to this?», he asked Maddy. «Who is ‹Berlin Enterprises›?»

«We are», she said.

He looked at her unbelievingly and laughed. «What do you want, then?»

«An explanation», said Sakina.

«An explanation of what?» He was still smiling.

«An explanation why you don't want your son to be seen on European television», said Maddy.

Gary Korbel looked around. «Well, we can't talk here. Why don't we go to a small café I know nearby. We won't be disturbed there.»

Maddy, Manni, Sakina, Una and Florian followed him to the door. He turned around. «Are all five of you going to come along? Christ, it's like taking a bunch of kids on a school trip.»

«I'm sure it's much more entertaining than that», grinned Una.

Dabei könnten wir sogar sechs sein, dachte Manni. Der arme Henk verpasst jetzt vielleicht das Wichtigste. Aber einer musste in Reserve bleiben, man wusste ja nie, was passieren konnte.

«Right. Where do you want me to begin?», Gary Korbel asked after they had ordered something to drink.

«Well you shouldn't begin with a story about Andy being sick in hospital because we know that's not true», said Maddy.

«And it's no use trying to tell us that he was removed from the series because you own the production company which makes ‹Superchain›», added Sakina.

Richtig so, Sakina, immer voll drauf, dachte Florian. Er darf gar nicht zur Besinnung kommen. Erst das Medien-Spektakel und ihm jetzt gleich die Ausreden wegnehmen, so fühlt er sich in die Enge getrieben.

«Why don't you just tell us why you don't want Andy to be seen on television in Europe?», Una said.

«You seem to have been doing a lot of homework», Gary Korbel said, nodding his head slowly, «but why do you think I should tell you anything? I could just tell you to mind your own business and you couldn't do anything about it.»

«We could sell the story and the information we have so far to one of your rival newspapers. I'm sure they would be very interested», sagte Florian. Jawohl, voll drauf. Die Antwort hatten sie sich gestern Abend schon ausgedacht und Florian hatte sie auswendig gelernt. Korbel sollte von allen fünf bombardiert werden. Wie in einem Verhör. Schade, dass wir ihn nicht mit einem starken Licht blenden können. Florians Phantasie ging mit ihm durch.

«Okay, you've won», admitted Gary Korbel. «Publicity about the affair is the last thing I want. You will see why when I tell you the story.» He stopped to take a sip of coffee and then continued. «Why don't you tell me exactly how much you know first?»

«No. We invited you here to do the telling», Una was firm.

Gary Korbel gave an irritated smile. «You want to know why I don't want Andy to be seen on European television? It's a long story and a confidential one. Can I trust you to keep your mouth shut afterwards?»

Fünffaches Kopfnicken. Von wegen, dachte Manni dabei, erst mal wollen wir wissen, was er uns nun wieder für eine Geschichte auftischt.

«You might know that I used to be a foreign correspondent for the newspaper I now own. Foreign correspondents are very useful people. For their governments, I mean. They have a press card, have access to places, people and information which a member of the general public doesn't have, and most important of all, they always have a good reason for asking questions and keeping their eyes open. Do you get what I mean?» He looked from one face to the other. Manni und Maddy nickten, Sakina und Una runzelten die Stirn, und Florians Gesicht war ein einziges Fragezeichen. Immerhin, dachte Manni, dass er Auslandskorrespondent war, stimmt. Bis jetzt sagt er die Wahrheit.

«I was doing some undercover work for the British government while I was abroad», he explained.

«While you were in Berlin?», fragte Florian. Erst als ihm das rausgerutscht war, erinnerte er sich daran, dass sie ihn alles erzählen lassen wollten, ohne anzudeuten, was sie schon wussten. Er hätte sich treten können.

«So you knew I was in Berlin», Gary Korbel said. «Yes, I did a lot of valuable work for Her Majesty's Government while I was there. The only problem with that kind of work is that when the results are evident it is usually obvious who was collecting the information. I couldn't risk my life by going back there today.»

Florian verstand das alles nicht und bat Sakina, Manni und Maddy, ihm das doch auf Deutsch zu erklären. Una now wished for the first time in her life that she could understand German. She wouldn't mind hearing a clearer explanation of what Andy's father was saying.

«That's all very understandable», said Maddy, «but it still doesn't explain why Andy shouldn't appear on television in Europe.»

«You have seen Andy», said his father, «you will have noticed how like me he looks. If he is seen by someone who had something to do with me all those years ago, it might jog their memory. And the consequences of that mightn't be all that pleasant.»

Es herrschte andächtige Stille. Die, die verstanden hatten, worum es ging, schwiegen. Die, die es nicht verstanden hatten, wollten sich nicht blamieren, indem sie etwas sagten. Endlich redete Gary Korbel weiter.

«Now you will understand why this whole affair was hushed up. It was unfortunate that Andy applied to take part in ‹Super-chain› without talking to me first, but once the damage was done it had to be undone quickly and quietly.»

‹Quickly› and ‹quietly› war das, das musste man ihm lassen, dachte Manni. Warum Stephen Robinson und Ginger Marley denn mitgemacht hatten, wollte er wissen.

«Stephen and I studied together. We are good friends. I was lucky that it happened to be one of his shows. He told all his staff the ‹hospital› story. Only Ginger knew the whole lot. She had found out that Andy was my son. She said she needed a bit of help with her career. You see, in my position one has quite a bit of influence. One can decide who should be the host of what show, for example. As a matter of fact I'll be in the studio to-morrow – not just to watch your final, even though I'm looking forward to seeing you win, but also to sign Ginger up for a new show which Stephen's and my company will produce together. One which will be on TV every Saturday evening. Entertainment for all the family. It's a real step forward for her career. Do you understand?»

Manni nickte. Das verstand er sehr gut. Er hatte schließlich mit eigenen Augen gesehen, wie Ginger Marley plötzlich zur Gastgeberin einer Bühnenshow geworden war. Das war also ihr Probelauf gewesen. All das machte Andys Vater nicht gerade sympathischer. Der schien seine Gedanken erraten zu haben, denn er sagte:

«I know at your age it is hard to accept these things, but you know the German saying ‹Eine Hand wäscht die andere›, don't you? Let me tell you – it's absolutely true.»

Er hat Recht, dachte Manni, *it's hard to accept*, und ich will es nicht akzeptieren.

Gary Korbel ließ sich die Rechnung geben. Er sah sie einen nach dem anderen durchdringend an und sagte pathetisch: «Look, nothing has happened. No damage has been done to anybody. No one would have known if you hadn't noticed the change. I congratulate you on your powers of observation and investigation and, as someone who used those same powers in the services of his country, I appeal to you to leave the matter stand where it is. Don't ask any more questions and please don't say a word about all this to anyone else. Can I have your word on that?»

«Yes», said four voices, although two of them weren't sure what they were agreeing to. That man had an amazing way with words. Gary Korbel looked at Manni who had remained silent.

«Won't you give me your word as well», he asked, «your *Ehrenwort*?»

«Okay», antwortete er. Wohl war ihm dabei nicht.

Sechzehntes Kapitel

****

in dem ein Fax die Wende bringt
and in which Maddy dances with a vampire

Henk had nothing to report when he arrived back late at the Butler's house. After Andy's father had left the café he had gone straight home.

Alle sechs saßen da und wussten nicht so recht, was sie tun sollten. Gary Korbel hatte Recht, niemand war geschädigt worden, abgesehen vielleicht von Andy. Sie hatten den Fall gelöst. Aber bei keinem der sechs hatte das zu einer besonders guten Laune geführt.

«So that was it», sagte Maddy, «a media boss who once worked for the secret service.»

Ein Medienboss, der offensichtlich unter einer Art Verfolgungswahn litt, dachte Manni. Warum sonst würde er glauben, dass man ihn durch seinen Sohn erkennen würde? Vor allem, wo im Fernsehen nie ihre Nachnamen genannt wurden; sie wurden immer einfach nur mit ‹Henk›, ‹Andy› usw. angeredet. Wieder saßen sie einige Zeit nur rum.

«This is ridiculous», said Una, «tomorrow the three of you could win a super trip to New York and Florida and we are sitting around here like a month of rainy Sundays just because the big media monster didn't murder his grandmother or anything like that. Come on, let's put on some music and play a round of Trivial Pursuit. That way Maddy can think she's preparing herself for the final.»

Una hatte Recht. Langsam lockerte sich die Stimmung. Und als Sakina und Henk, die als Erste die Mitte der Spielfläche erreicht hatten, von den anderen dort mit Sportfragen aufgehalten wurden, ging es ganz schön turbulent zu.

«Good luck pet», Maddy's mother gave her a kiss goodbye the next morning, «pity I can't be there, but remember, winning isn't everything. I'll be just as proud of you even if you don't win.» Oh God. Maddy knew her mother meant well, but she shouldn't slobber over her like that in front of people.

Florian begleitete Maddy bis zur Gartentür, wo Joannes Auto auf sie wartete. Dort machte er viele kleine Kussgeräusche und sagte: «Auch ich bin stolz auf dich, Haustier, wenn du nicht gewinnst.»

Maddy gave him a punch in the stomach. «That'll teach you to make fun of me», she said.

Florian lachte nur. «Toi, toi, toi», rief er ihr nach, und «wir sehen uns heute Nachmittag im Studio.»

She smiled and waved. «Thanks. See you later.»

Florian ging ins Haus zurück. «Why aren't you going with her?», wollte Maddys Mutter von ihm wissen.

«There are only rehearsals in the morning, Mrs Butler, Sakina, Una and I will go there in a few hours' time.»

Zwei Stunden später rief Mr Butler an. Ein Fax war angekommen. Es schien sich um Zeitungsausschnitte zu handeln. Die könne er leider nicht am Telefon vorlesen, da er kein Deutsch spreche. Florian rief Sakina und Una an und verabredete sich mit ihnen in Mr Butlers Büro. Hatte Silvia etwas gefunden? Sie holten das Fax ab, warteten aber, bis sie draußen waren, bevor sie es sich genauer ansahen. Es handelte sich in der Tat um zwei Zeitungsartikel. Florian verschlang den ersten.

KINDESENTFÜHRUNG

Berlin-Charlottenburg.
Harald, das sechsmonatige Baby von Edith Holst, ist gestern entführt worden. Edith Holst war am Samstagabend mit einer Freundin im Kino gewesen. Gary Korbel, Berlin-Korrespondent einer großen Londoner Tageszeitung und Vater des Kindes, hatte auf das Kind aufgepasst. Edith Holst und Gary Korbel hatten sich schon vor einem Jahr getrennt – einvernehmlich, wie beide betonen. Und wie schon öfter hatte Gary Babysitter gespielt, wenn Edith, eine attraktive Blondine in den Zwanzigern, abends ausging. «Ich habe nur am Automaten Zigaretten geholt, vielleicht habe ich die Tür offen gelassen», sagte der Vater. Er wirkte sehr niedergeschlagen. Die Polizei hat noch keine Spur. Auch Lösegeldforderungen wurden bisher noch nicht gestellt.

«Das ist ja ein Ding», entfuhr es Florian, als er den Artikel gelesen hatte.

«Come on, come on, what does it say?», demanded Una impatiently.

Florian versuchte den Text zu übersetzen. Aber das klappte überhaupt nicht. So sagte er: «Gary Korbel and a woman called Edith Holst had a baby in Berlin. A boy – Harald. The baby was six months old. It was kidnapped when Gary was babysitting.»

«Wow!», said Una. «Do you think Andy could be the kidnapped baby in question?»

«Maybe, maybe not», said Sakina, «he could have been born after all this happened.»

Florian las den zweiten Artikel. Er war drei Wochen danach erschienen und kürzer. Unter der Überschrift ‹KEINE SPUR VON BABY HARALD› stand, dass man immer noch nichts von den Kidnappern gehört habe und dass die Polizei ratlos sei. Die Eltern seien sehr besorgt, endete der Artikel, und hätten eine Belohnung ausgesetzt.

«How odd», said Una after Florian had summed up what was in the article, «what do you think? Is Andy Korbel ‹Baby Harald›?»

«We have to contact him straight away», said Sakina, «that's the only way we'll find out.»

An sich hätten die drei Jugglers jetzt auf dem Weg ins Studio sein müssen, wenn sie das Finale ganz miterleben wollten. Aber die Sache mit Andy war noch wichtiger. Zum Glück war er zu Hause, als sie ihn anriefen und sagten, sie müssten unbedingt mit ihm sprechen. Florian bestand darauf, mit dem Taxi zu fahren, obwohl alle drei eine Travelcard hatten. Die Zeit sei zu knapp für U-Bahn und Bus, falls sie anschließend doch was vom Finale mitbekommen wollten, behauptete er. Florian fuhr sehr gern und viel zu wenig Taxi und freute sich, dass er endlich einen triftigen Grund dafür hatte. Er lud die beiden Mädchen dazu ein.

When the rehearsal started it was not Rosemary but one of the other production assistants who stood in for Ginger.

«Where's Rosemary?», fragte Manni Derek während einer der Unterbrechungen.

«Not here. Rumour has it that she has been sacked.»

«Sacked?» Manni verstand das Wort nicht.

Derek musste seine Nachfrage wohl als Ausruf der Empörung verstanden haben, denn er sagte: «Yes, sacked, just like that. There's no justice in the world.»

«Fired», kam Maddy Manni zu Hilfe; sie hatte sein Nachfragen richtig verstanden. Fired? Rausgeschmissen? Weil sie auf dem Proben-Band war, das sie gestern im MOMI gespielt hatten? Maddy felt herself getting very angry.

They would have to talk to Gary Korbel again. But first they had to concentrate on winning the show. Especially as they would have to beat the Argonauts to do so!

Der Vormittag verlief quälend langsam. Nach der Probe kam Stephen Robinson, der *Executive Producer*, ins Studio hinunter und wünschte allen viel Glück. «Everything sorted out?», he said to the Floppies. They nodded.

«Except for one thing», Maddy remembered, «a certain lady who isn't here in the studio this morning shouldn't have to pay for other people's mistakes, should she?»

Stephen Robinson paused for a second. «I'll think about it», he replied before he went back upstairs to the gallery.

Endlich war es dann so weit. Eröffnungsfanfare. Auftritt Ginger Marley. Sie hatte sich für das Finale besonders elegant angezogen.

«Here we are», she said, «after seven Qualifying Rounds, one Consolation Match, four Quarterfinals and two Semifinals we have now reached the Grand Final. The Argonauts against the Floppies. Let's have a look at how they got here.»

Auf dem Bildschirm wurde jetzt der Spielverlauf eingeblendet und Ginger schaltete ihr Lächeln einen Gang runter. Aber ihre Stimme blieb süß und freundlich: «In the very first match of our series the Argonauts won against the Jugglers. As you can see on our winner board, they then won their way through to the finals by beating the Tigers and the Fanclub. Here they are: Carla, David and Andy – the Argonauts!» Ginger schaltete ihr Lächeln wieder auf volle Stärke.

Endlich ging es los. Die Floppies hatten sich entschlossen, diesmal ihre unschlagbare Kombination bis zur letzten Runde

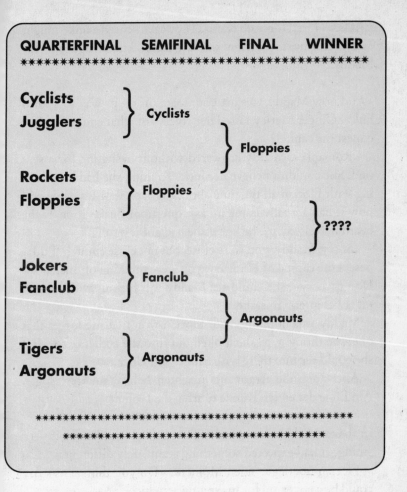

QUARTERFINAL	SEMIFINAL	FINAL	WINNER

Cyclists
Jugglers
} Cyclists

} Floppies

Rockets
Floppies
} Floppies

} ????

Jokers
Fanclub
} Fanclub

} Argonauts

Tigers
Argonauts
} Argonauts

aufzusparen: Henk für den Bereich Wissen, Maddy für den Bereich Geschicklichkeit und Manni für den Bereich Potpourri. Daher übernahm in der ersten Runde Maddy den Bereich Wissen, für den sie die ganze Zeit gelernt hatte, Manni den Geschicklichkeitsbereich und Henk das Potpourri.

It began well for both teams. They each scored a link straight away. The next question was a general knowledge one for Maddy.

«And now Maddy, to start your team off on its way to a third link», Ginger Marley raised her voice, «of what country is Budapest the capital?»

«Romania», Maddy answered without hesitating for a second. She couldn't believe her luck. To think she had been joking with Florian all the time about the capital of Romania and now it had actually come up as a question. But as soon as she heard herself say it, she knew she had got it wrong.

«Sorry, Maddy, you were close, but not close enough. Budapest is the capital of Hungary, you were thinking of Bucharest. Don't worry», she could see Maddy was furious with herself, «it is a common mistake.»

Maddy was hopping mad. Florian won't let me forget that one, she thought, as she looked out into the audience to see if she could see him there with Sakina and Una.

Aber auch die Argonauts machten Fehler, mehrere sogar. Am Ende der ersten Runde führten die Floppies 3 : 2.

In the taxi Sakina remarked: «That Baby Harald story is very strange. I had expected something completely different.»

Florian überlegte einen Moment. «Do you think this story could be a cover-up for his spying activity?»

Sakina hadn't thought about that. «I don't know. But I would imagine that if he was involved in secret service work then he wouldn't want any sort of publicity at all.»

«She's right», agreed Una. «Look, there's one way of finding out a bit more. We can simply ask Andy about his mother.»

The film title which had to be mimed, drawn and guessed in the Round 2 was ‹Dance of the Vampires›. That's easy enough, thought Maddy as she held up four fingers to tell Manni it was a title with four words. The third word was ‹the›. She told him this by making a ‹T› with her fingers. It was a sign they had agreed on earlier. Now she was going to show him the first word.

«Disco!», rief er, als sie um ihn herumtanzte.

She shook her head.

«Party?... Rock and roll?... Music!»

If the word was ‹music› I would play a bloody musical instrument, wouldn't I, said Maddy to herself. Was he totally stupid? She was annoyed and her movements became stiffer.

Mensch, du siehst doch, dass ich auf'm falschen Dampfer bin, ärgerte sich Manni, kannst du es nicht anders versuchen? Er probierte eine andere Richtung: «Are you boxing? It is one of those ‹Rocky› films?»

Maddy raised her eyes to heaven. He was all wrong.

«You aren't flying again, are you?», versuchte er es verzweifelt noch einmal.

This was hopeless. Maddy stopped dancing altogether for a second. Then she pretended to ask her partner to dance with her and she waltzed with him around the studio floor.

«It's a waltz!» Na klar, dachte Manni, das ist es. Was für Filme mit ‹Walzer› im Titel kannte er? O Gott, das waren sicher alles Filme, die seine Oma gesehen hatte.

Maddy made a sign to him to wait a moment. Then she did what she thought looked like a few steps of a Highland Fling. She hoped her grandfather would forgive her when he saw it on the TV in Edinburgh. Then she stopped again and went back to disco dancing. Surely he must be able to guess it now.

«Dancing... dance», rief Manni endlich. Seine Stimme klang enttäuscht. Darauf hätte er ja nun auch schon eher kommen können.

Maddy moved on to the more difficult word, ‹vampires› but to her great surprise, Manni guessed it as soon as she pointed to her eye teeth, drawing them down to make them into long fangs.

‹Dance – the Vampires›, so weit hatte er es, aber er kannte keinen Film, der so hieß. Was war das zweite Wort? *Dance* irgendwas the *Vampires*. Irgendeine Präposition vielleicht? – Dance with the Vampires, Dance without the Vampires, Dance for the Vampires, Dance to the Vampires, Dance beside the Vampires, Dance between the Vampires, Dance above the Vampires – rasselte er herunter, bis er die richtige traf: Dance of the Vampires!

Manni ärgerte sich über sich. Das war viel zu langsam. Hoffentlich reagierte Henk besser auf seine Zeichnungen.

Manni looked exhausted. Would they still make it, Maddy worried. Henk had guessed ‹Vampires› already and Manni was just drawing a lot of them together when she heard a roar of applause from the audience. The Argonauts were finished. Don't give up, Maddy pleaded silently, we need to get it finished in good time to still get a link or two. Within seconds Henk had guessed the title of the film. Well done. Each team got two links for finishing quickly and the Argonauts got an extra one for winning the round. Now it was level: 5 all.

Als Florian, Una und Sakina bei Andy ankamen, wollten sie ihn nicht gleich mit ihren Neuigkeiten überfallen. Sie grüßten und fragten ihn, wie es ihm ergangen war, seit sie ihn im Park getroffen hatten. Er hatte nichts Neues zu berichten. Nach wie vor weigerte sich sein Vater, eine Erklärung für sein Handeln zu geben.

«And what does your mother say about the whole thing?», Una asked innocently.

«Oh, she's in the States producing a film», he said, «she left four weeks ago.»

«Is she American?» Wieder musste Florian Unas kaltblütige Art bewundern.

«No, Australian.»

«You mightn't have anything to tell us, but we have lots to tell you», Sakina said. Die drei fingen an, Teile von dem zu berichten, was sie bis dahin erlebt und herausgefunden hatten.

Andy was amazed at the stories which had been told about him and his father. «Derek said I was in hospital?», he asked unbelievingly and «Why would Ginger Marley tell you a story like that about my father owning the production company? He owns lots of them but not that particular one, believe it or not. It's not true and well she knows it. That one belongs to Stephen Robinson, a friend of my father's.» He frowned. «I am half afraid to find out whatever my father's reason is», he said, «so many people are involved in the cover-up that it must be something serious. Do you know anything else?»

Die drei fielen sich ständig ins Wort, als sie von ihrem Auftreten im MOMI berichteten. «We wanted to beat him at his own media game», giggled Una. «You should have seen his face!», she added.

«So he was a spy!», Andy said when they finally finished telling him about the MOMI set up and the conversation in the café. «Why didn't he tell me? I would have thought it was something to be proud of, to boast to your son about. Why all the hush-hush?»

Keiner der drei sagte etwas. Andy sah unruhig von einem zum anderen.

«Is there something you haven't told me?» Seine Stimme klang unsicher.

In Mannis Magen kribbelte es. Nun kam die dritte Runde, die am wenigsten berechenbar war: ‹wahr oder falsch›. Man konnte nicht einmal vorher absprechen, welchen Knopf alle drei im Zweifelsfall drücken sollten, um eine 50 : 50-Chance zu haben, denn wenn alle eine falsche Antwort gaben, bedeutete das den Verlust eines Glieds der Kette.

«And now for the first statement», begann Ginger Marley. «The average man of today will spend almost 3500 hours of his life in front of a mirror, shaving – true or false?» Manni versuchte gar nicht erst zu rechnen, es war hoffnungslos. Er drückte instinktiv auf den ‹true›-Knopf. So einen Blödsinn kann sich keiner ausdenken. Alle anderen hatten offensichtlich dasselbe gedacht, denn Ginger verkündete:

«Nobody was fooled by that one. In front of me I see six votes for ‹true›. And true it is. Each team gets one link.»

Immer noch stand es unentschieden: 6 : 6.

«Our second statement: There are now about 12 000 Indian restaurants in London. This is a true fact», las Ginger Marley vor. «Is it true or false to say that 50 years ago there were only 40?» Das weiß Sakina bestimmt, durchfuhr es Manni. Sie müsste hinter den Scheinwerfern unter den Zuschauern sein. Aber er hatte sie, Florian und Una noch gar nicht gesehen. Manni tippte auf ‹false›. Es gab schon damals bestimmt mehr indische Restaurants.

«Well, we have very clear results here. The Floppies all think that the statement is false and the Argonauts believe that it's

174

true. That means one team will gain a link, the others will lose one. Who will it be?»

Nun sag's doch endlich, dachte Manni. Die blöde Zicke will es für die Fernsehzuschauer spannender machen, dabei konnte er es vor Spannung kaum noch aushalten.

«The statement was false. So the Floppies get a link, the Argonauts lose one. The score is 7 : 5, the Floppies are in the lead. But I am sure they thought that statement was false for the wrong reasons. The number 40 was not too small – believe it or not – it was too large. There were only 4 Indian restaurants in London 50 years ago.»

7 : 5 für uns. Manni fühlte sich erleichtert. Aber das änderte sich schnell. Bei zwei der drei folgenden Statements gaben alle Argonauts die korrekte Antwort, die Floppies gingen dagegen leer aus. 7 : 7 – wieder stand es unentschieden. Manni fühlte sich wieder ein wenig schlechter.

Florian zeigte Andy die Zeitungsausschnitte und erklärte, was drinstand. Andy wurde blass. «What does it mean! Do I have a brother I never knew about?»

Sollten sie ihm von ihrer Vermutung erzählen, dass er Baby Harald sein könnte, fragte sich Florian. Er sah zu Una und Sakina. Sakina was wondering, too.

«Andy», she asked slowly, «is your mother a real Australian or did she, em, did she...»

«She is called Miriam, not Edith, in case that's what you wanted to know», Andy interrupted her, «and she doesn't speak a word of German.»

Vielleicht tut sie nur so, als ob sie kein Deutsch sprechen könne, dachte Florian. Vielleicht hatten Edith Holst und Gary Korbel Baby Harald ja auf eine Weise zurückbekommen, die nicht legal war. Vielleicht hatten sie jemand dabei verletzt oder getötet und waren danach nach Australien geflohen. Oder vielleicht war das Baby auch ein paar Monate später gefunden worden und Silvia hatte bloß den Artikel darüber nicht gefunden. Aber warum durfte Andy dann nicht im Fernsehen auftreten? Weil jemandem die Ähnlichkeit von Andy und seinem Vater aufgefallen wäre? Weil dieser Jemand dann einen Fall, den alle vergessen hatten oder vergessen wollten, wieder in die Zeitungen gebracht hätte? Florian fragte die anderen.

«I don't know», Una said, «even if he had hit the kidnapper over the head – wouldn't he have had the right to do it?»

«There's only one way to find out about the whole business», said Andy who had felt very uncomfortable while Florian and Una were speculating about his father, «we'll have to ask him – now!»

«No problem», antwortete Florian und gab ihm die vierte Eintrittskarte, die Maddy angeblich für ihre Mutter bestellt hatte, obwohl sie wusste, dass die sicher nicht hingehen konnte, weil sie arbeitete. Maddys sechster Sinn! «If we go to the studio now, he'll be there», sagte er.

Chapter seventeen

****

about which nothing will be told in advance

Die letzte Runde. 7 : 7. Es wurde ausgelost, wer zuerst spielen musste. Es erwischte die Argonauts. Sie entschieden sich erst mal für eine normale Aufgabe. Carla beantwortete ihre Wissensfrage korrekt, ihr folgte David mit einem erfolgreichen Wurf auf das Darts-Brett.

That's not fair, thought Maddy, he had to do that in the very first match he played, too, and he's really good at it. Andy completed his task without any problem at all. The Argonauts had gone into the lead 8 : 7.

So Maddy thought, it looks like we should go for a risk question. «Risk», said Henk as if he had read her thoughts. He stared at the subjects left on the display board… oh no, the light stopped at ‹pop music›.

Oh God, thought Maddy, of all the sub-categories which belonged to general knowledge, pop music was guaranteed to be the one where Henk had the least idea. She cursed silently. Why hadn't she got that in the first round? Did that mean their chance of victory was gone?

Ginger read the question: «In the concerts of which pop singer is a free fall into the audience a regular feature?»

Manni hätte fast laut gelacht. Eine Peter-Gabriel-Frage war gestern Abend aufgetaucht, als sie Trivial Pursuit gespielt hatten; und dann hatten sie über dessen Show geredet.

«Peter Gabriel», said Henk. He was right. Sheer luck. The

Floppies were on their way again. Following Henk's example, Maddy and Manni were also successful. They were now in the lead. 9 : 8. The three Floppies looked at each other and smiled.

In der zweiten Runde gingen die Argonauts nicht mehr auf Sicherheit und wählten die Risikofragen. Hätte ich auch gemacht, dachte Manni.

Maddy had to stop herself biting her nails after Carla answered her question with no problem at all and David completed his skill task in record time. Hopefully Andy will get his mixed bag task wrong, she thought, but he hadn't the slightest bit of difficulty. 10 : 9 for the Argonauts. We can say goodbye to Florida if we don't get our double link in this round, Maddy thought sadly.

Warum musste Henk ausgerechnet Popmusik erwischen? Bei fast allen anderen Gebieten wäre er erstklassig gewesen. Aber Popmusik? Doch als Manni die Frage hörte, die Ginger stellte, konnte er kaum glauben, was für ein Glück sie wieder hatten.

«Which Dutch city housed a pop radio station which was listened to in the 1960s by lots of young people all over Europe?»

«Hilversum», Henk answered immediately.

Ginger laughed. «That's the way the questions sometimes come. A Dutch question for a Dutch contestant. What luck!»

Maddy closed her eyes. It was her turn now. She took a deep breath. She was led out to the centre of the studio floor. There she was shown a shape which was drawn on a huge white sheet of paper. It looked like a giant ice-cube or something. She was only allowed to study it for about 5 seconds. Then it was taken away. She wondered what she would be asked to do now. Draw it? Guess what it was? Guess its size? She was led over to

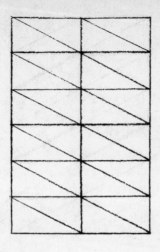

a kind of stand. On it a was another large sheet of paper onto which oblong boxes, two wide, six long, each with a diagonal line through it were drawn. Maddy had to insert the shape she had just seen onto the pattern now before her.

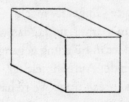

She had 25 seconds in which to do it. Das schafft sie nie, dachte Manni. Bye, bye, Florida. Zu seinem großen Erstaunen schaffte es Maddy jedoch in der vorgegebenen Zeit. Nun waren sie wieder auf dem Weg zum Ausgleich. Alles hing jetzt an ihm.

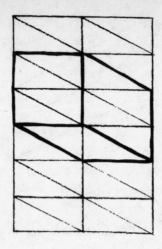

Seine Potpourri-Aufgabe bestand darin, zwei von drei Titel-melodien von Fernsehserien zu identifizieren. Endlich mal was Leichtes, dachte er. Die Musik spielte. ‹Miami Vice› konnte er sofort identifizieren, danach kam... Die Melodie kannte er schon, woher bloß? Das war... das muss doch... Nein, er konnte es nicht identifizieren. So ein Mist.

«Neighbours», sagte Ginger... macht nichts, eine durfte er auslassen... jetzt kam's drauf an, ja, das war ‹Dallas›. Hurra. 11 : 10. Sie waren wieder in Führung gegangen.

«Stop», unterbrach der Aufnahmeleiter, «I'm afraid we have to take a ten minutes' break now. We're having problems with one of the cameras.»

Der *warm-up man* begann, den Zuschauern Witze zu erzäh-len. Dieselben wie beim Halbfinale. Und beim Viertelfinale. Und und und. Manni versuchte, gegen das Scheinwerferlicht im Zuschauerraum Una, Sakina und Florian zu erkennen. Wo steckten die bloß?

Maddy was pleased. They had a real chance of winning the final. She looked into the audience. Where were the others? There! They had only just come in. With – with Andy? What had kept them? And why was Andy with them? Jetzt hatten auch Henk und Manni die vier entdeckt. Sie gingen direkt auf Gary Korbel zu, der sich gerade mit Ginger Marley unterhielt. Manni sah, wie Andy Florian ein Stück Papier aus der Hand nahm und es seinem Vater vor die Augen hielt. What's on the paper, Maddy wondered. Could it be a fax? Florian had phoned that journalist friend of his in Berlin the day before yesterday. Had she found something out? Maddy started to walk over to them. So did Henk and Manni. Florian sah Manni, Henk und Maddy zu ihnen herüberkommen, aber seine ganze Aufmerksamkeit galt Andys Vater. Wie würde er reagieren?

Gary Korbel looked at the newspaper articles, looked at Andy, at Florian, Una and Sakina and then said in a tired voice to Ginger: «Ginger, love, could I use your changing-room? I think I have to talk to these four…», he saw Henk, Maddy and Manni coming towards him, «…to these seven in private.» Ginger gave him her best smile. «Of course, if you all manage to fit in. You know where it is, don't you?»

Auf dem Weg zu Gingers Garderobe informierte Florian die Floppies schnell über den Zeitungsartikel. Gary Korbel sagte, dass er lieber zuerst allein mit Andy reden wollte. Manni fand das richtig und wollte gerade zustimmen, als er Andy antworten hörte: «No, you have tried to fool them just as you have tried to fool me. We want to know – all of us – and we want to know now.» Manni bemerkte den kalten Blick, den Andy seinem Vater zuwarf.

Als sie sich alle in das schmale Zimmer gedrängt hatten, begann Gary Korbel.

«Andy, please try to understand. It was all in your best interest. You must believe me, please.»

Es war, als ob die anderen im Augenblick für ihn gar nicht existierten. Andy reagierte nicht. Er starrte seinen Vater nur an. Gary Korbel griff nach einer Zigarette.

«I had an affair with Edith Holst in Berlin, not for very long – on and off, really. Then I met Miriam, your mother, Andy.» Die ganze Betonung lag auf *mother*. «It was love at first sight. We met in Cologne where she was working for a business associate of her father's. Soon we planned to get married. In Australia where her family was. I got in touch with our London head office and they promised to make me their correspondent in Sydney soon afterwards.»

Aha, dachte Florian, das erklärt, warum er Korrespondent in Australien wurde. So weit stimmte das also. Gary Korbel continued.

«Of course I broke it off with Edith straight away. A few weeks later I heard that she was pregnant.» Er hielt inne und sah die anderen der Reihe nach an. «Please promise to keep all this to yourselves, for my sake and especially for Andy's sake.» Besonders lange ruhten seine Augen auf Manni. So kam es dem jedenfalls vor. Sollte er darauf antworten? Aber schon antwortete Andy: «I'll decide what's good and what isn't good for my sake. Now I just want to know what happened.»

«The baby was born», fuhr sein Vater fort, «a healthy little boy. Edith called him Harald. She changed a lot after birth. She started treating me, created scenes, started drinking heavily and went out a lot. I spent quite some time looking after the baby.»

Davon stand nichts in der Zeitung, dachte Florian. Aber der Mann hatte ihnen schon so viele Geschichten erzählen lassen und erzählt, vielleicht arbeitete er ja gerade wieder an einer neuen Ausrede. Sie sollten jetzt offensichtlich alle Mitleid mit ihm haben, weil diese Edith so böse war.

«Andy, what I have to say now is very painful, for you and for me», wandte er sich direkt an seinen Sohn, «please let's talk about this alone together.»

Andy schüttelte den Kopf. Gary Korbel zog an seiner Zigarette und fuhr fort. «One day it happened. Miriam phoned. She had just found out that she could never have a child.»

Sechs Augenpaare wanderten von Andys Vater zu Andy. Der saß da, kreidebleich. Bewegte die Lippen, brachte aber keinen Ton hervor.

«I am sorry, Andy», sagte Gary Korbel. Er machte eine Bewegung, als wolle er seinen Sohn in die Arme nehmen. Aber er tat es nicht. Stattdessen sprach er weiter: «I suppose you can guess the rest. It was my idea and Miriam agreed. One day, when Edith was off on one of her drinking sessions again, Miriam took the baby and left Berlin. She went by train through East Germany, and by boat to Copenhagen. From there she took the plane to Australia. A few hours after she had left I went to the police and told my story. That I had just gone to get some cigarettes and so on. They searched all over Berlin, checked all the West German borders, airports and so on, without any success. After a few months the whole affair died down. I left for Australia, Miriam and I got married and we got a false birth certificate for Andy. With a little help from my father-in-law I got into the media business, bought some production companies, got rich... And the three of us lived happily ever after. But of course as far as Edith, her friends and the German authorities are concerned there is still the open case of the missing baby. So you can understand my horror when I found out that Andy was in a TV show which could be seen in Berlin.»

Manni konnte das sehr gut nachvollziehen. Was für eine Geschichte. Andy von seinem eigenen Vater gekidnappt. Henk, Sakina, Florian, Una und Maddy saßen mit betretenen Gesichtern da. Keiner zweifelte daran, dass es diesmal die richtige Erklärung war. Es war zu schrecklich.

Andy zitterte am ganzen Leib. «I want to go to Berlin to find my mother», stieß er unter Tränen hervor.

«Andy, your mother is in the States. *Miriam is* your mother. Your real mother. She loves you. She brought you up.» Gary Korbel versuchte, seinen Sohn zu umarmen. Der stieß ihn weg.

«Leave me alone», schrie er und rannte, über Sakina hinweg-stolpernd, zur Tür hinaus. Gary Korbel sprang auf und lief hinterher. Dabei rannte er fast Derek um, der von Ginger geschickt worden war, um zu sagen, dass es weitergehen konnte.

«Hey, what's happening here?», he said cheerfully. For a few seconds nobody reacted then Maddy laughed thinly. «Nothing much», she said, «we just wanted to find out how many people would fit into this tiny room.» Derek gave her a funny look.

«Ist das okay, wenn wir einfach weitermachen?», Maddy asked the others in German which Derek didn't understand. It was good that Ginger had sent Derek and not Joanne. Manni und Henk nickten. *The show must go on*, dachte Manni; jetzt mussten Andy und sein Vater miteinander klarkommen. Mein Gott, noch drei richtige Antworten bis Florida, und statt auf Hochspannung zu sein, waren sie alle ziemlich geschafft.

«Come on, Floppies, now that we're here you'll just have to win», Una tried to cheer them up.

«Okay», gab Manni zurück, «but you'll have to... squeeze your thumbs.»

Una hadn't a clue what he meant.

«Hier drücken sie nicht die Daumen, sondern kreuzen die

Finger», belehrte Florian Manni. «You should cross your fingers», sagte er zu Una.

«I'll try to squeeze my thumbs and keep my fingers crossed at the same time if it helps», Una decided.

11 : 10 für die Floppies. Die Argonauts mussten natürlich auf Risiko gehen und sie taten es mit Bravour. Zwei neue Glieder leuchteten auf der Kette auf. 12 : 11 für die Argonauts. Während die Argonauts dran waren, hatte Manni ins Publikum gesehen. Er versuchte, gegen das Scheinwerferlicht Florian, Una und Sakina unter den Zuschauern zu erkennen. Keine Spur von Andy oder seinem Vater. Aber er meinte sogar zu erkennen, wie Una eine Hand hochhielt – bestimmt mit gedrücktem Daumen und gekreuzten Fingern, dachte er und lachte innerlich. Jetzt musste er sich auf die letzten drei Aufgaben konzentrieren. Was passierte eigentlich bei einem Unentschieden? Gab es ein Stechen? Nein, erinnerte er sich, die Mannschaft, die in der ersten und vierten Runde mehr richtige Antworten gegeben hatte, würde dann gewonnen haben. Das waren die anderen. Ein Unentschieden nützte also nichts. Sie mussten auf Risiko gehen. Und das hieß, Henk musste noch eine Risiko-Pop-Frage überleben. O je!

«From which rainy British city – recently cultural capital of Europe – does the group ‹Wet Wet Wet› come from?», Ginger Marley asked Henk.

Glasgow natürlich, dachte Manni. Aber woher sollte Henk das wissen? Der hatte bestimmt noch nie was von ‹Wet Wet Wet› gehört.

«Glasgow», said Henk, after a moment's hesitation. He had never heard of ‹Wet Wet Wet›. But he had seen a documentary about Glasgow as the cultural capital of Europe the week before. The audience clapped. Maddy heard a few roars of ‹hooray› and looked up to see Una clapping and waving. Florian and Sakina were clapping and cheering as well. She must get her task right, she said to herself, she didn't want to lose the prize for the team.

She was led to a small table on which mixed coloured beads and five coloured sticks were placed. There were five beads each of the colours red, blue, yellow, green and orange. She had to put them onto the five different coloured sticks – red bead on red stick etc. – using one hand only. She wasn't allowed to put all five of one colour onto one stick and then move on to the next, there had to be one bead on each stick before she could put a second one on anywhere, and so on. Just don't think how long it's taking, she thought as she tried to calm herself down. Her hand was shaking and she dropped some of the beads. After a few seconds it got better, though. Red, blue, yellow, green, orange, she said to herself, concentrating on the order in which she was putting the beads on the sticks. Red, blue, yellow, green, orange. It was almost hypnotic. Before 90 seconds were over, she had completed the task to wild applause from the audience.

Mannis Knie zitterten. Nun hing alles von ihm ab. Hoffentlich konnte er seine Potpourri-Aufgabe lösen. Es wäre zu schlimm, wenn er sich blamieren und seine Mannschaft enttäuschen würde. Und das vor Abertausenden von Menschen in Europa. Auf einmal war ihm bewusst, wie viele ihn da draußen auf ihren Fernsehbildschirmen beobachten würden. Andys Vater hatte Recht. Irgendjemand in Berlin hätte Andy möglicherweise erkannt. Manni fühlte sich ganz, ganz schlecht. Er wäre am liebsten weggelaufen.

«And now Manni. Everything depends on you, you know», sagte Ginger Marley.

Er biss die Zähne zusammen. Weiß ich doch, du blöde Ziege, dachte er.

«Ready?», fuhr sie fort. «You've only got thirty seconds. If the numbers from 1 to 100, written in words, were arranged in alphabetic order, which would be the first five?»

Manni überlegte. Langsam antwortete er: «Eight... eighteen... eighty... eighty-eight... eighty-five... eighty...»

«Stop!», rief Ginger Marley, «I only wanted five. Well done, Manni, you have just earned your team a double link and with that the victory!»

Henk und Maddy fielen ihm um den Hals. Kaum zu glauben, das war's.

The audience were on their feet clapping and cheering. Ginger Marley was beaming into the camera saying «Ladies and gentlemen, here you see the winners of SUPERCHAIN – The Super European Quiz Show: the Floppies! Maddy from London, Henk from Utrecht and Manni from Berlin. They have just won themselves the superprize of a trip to New York and Florida.»

Loud music was playing, balloons appeared from nowhere, floating down from the studio ceiling. The Floppies were jumping for joy. The show was over. Dann sahen sie Gary Korbel auf sie zukommen. Er sah sehr ernst aus.

«Congratulations», sagte er, «what a magnificent victory.»

«Thanks», Maddy answered. «What about Andy?»

Gary Korbel sprach leiser. «We talked», sagte er, «and we are flying to Berlin tomorrow. He wants to talk to his real mother.» Seine Stimme klang jetzt sehr traurig. «Real mother. It was Miriam who brought him up, who loved him – he will realize that sooner or later. I suppose one always has to pay for what one has done.»

Manni nickte. Er wollte etwas sagen, aber ein Kloß steckte in seinem Hals.

«Anyway», Gary Korbel versuchte ein Lächeln, «I wish you – eh, what was it? – my German has gone a bit rusty – vielen Spaß in Florida.»

«Viel Spaß», Maddy corrected him automatically. Two pictures were in her mind at the same time. One was of all the sights, beaches, sun and all the fun they were going to have in Florida, the other was of Berlin and what would happen to Andy there. Poor Andy. Manni sah Maddy erstaunt an. Aus ihrem linken Auge kam eine Träne, und sie sah aus, als ob sie gleichzeitig weinte und lachte.

Emer O'Sullivan studierte in Dublin und Berlin Germanistik und Anglistik und arbeitet jetzt am Institut für Jugendbuchforschung der Universität Frankfurt/Main.
Dietmar Rösler arbeitet als Dozent im Department of German des King's College der University of London mit den Schwerpunkten Germanistik und Deutsch als Fremdsprache.

I like you – und du?

(rotfuchs 323/ab 12 Jahre)
Der irische Junge Paddy zieht nach Berlin und lernt dort Karin kennen. Aus der Not, daß er kaum Deutsch und sie schlecht Englisch kann, machen sie eine Tugend und kombinieren beides, so gut es geht. Der Leser hat, ehe er sich versieht, ein halbes Buch auf Englisch gelesen und viele Vokabeln gelernt - ganz ohne Wörterbuch.

It could be worse, oder?

(rotfuchs 374 / ab 13 Jahre)
Diesmal muß Karin sich in einer fremden Umgebung - in Irland - zurechtfinden, was ihr nicht leichtfällt. Steht die Freundschaft zwischen ihr und Paddy auf dem Spiel...?

Mensch, be careful!

(rotfuchs 417 / ab 13 Jahre)
Ein spannender Krimi in englisch-deutschem Sprachmischmasch über Juwelenschmuggel per Fisch!

Butler & Graf

(rotfuchs 480 / ab 14 Jahre)
Florian Graf, ein arroganter Junge aus reicher Familie, soll in London einen Sprachkurs mit «Familienanschluß» belegen. Maddy Butler, die Tochter der Familie, liebt Computer und Judo. Für Florian hat sie nicht viel übrig. Unvorhergesehen geraten beide in einen Kriminalfall, den sie gemeinsam deutsch-englisch aufzuklären versuchen.

Butler, Graf & Friends: Nur ein Spiel?

(rotfuchs 531 / ab 14 Jahre)
Ein deutsch-englischer Krimi über mysteriöse Ereignisse rund um ein Fernseh-Quiz...

Butler, Graf & Friends: Umwege

(rotfuchs 647 / ab 13 Jahre)
Maddy traut ihren Ohren nicht: Mannis Flugzeug soll nicht auf dem Flughafen, sondern auf der Autobahn landen. Die Durchsage erweist sich als falsch, doch die merkwürdigen Ereignisse nehmen kein Ende. Maddy und ihre Freunde versuchen, den Fall in bewährter deutsch-englischer Zusammenarbeit zu lösen.

rororo rotfuchs

Romane und Erzählungen
für Leser ab 9 Jahre.

Ghazi Abdel-Qudir
Mustafa mit dem Bauchladen
(20775 / ab 10 Jahre)
Eine Geschichte voller
Zuversicht um den elf-
jährigen Libanesen Mustafa.
Spannend, realistisch und
farbig erzählt.

Eva Bexell
**Kleine Schufte oder Das Klavier
brennt** *Besuch bei den
Großeltern*
(20835 / ab 9 Jahre)
Ein Lese- und Vorlese-
vergnügen für Großeltern,
Eltern, Kinder und Enkel!

Harald Grill
**Da kräht kein Hahn nach
dir** *Bernd zieht in die Stadt
Erzählung*
(20548 / ab 10 Jahre)

Max von der Grün
Vorstadtkrokodile *Eine Geschichte vom Aufpassen*
(20171 / ab 9 Jahre)
Nur wer eine gefährliche
Mutprobe bestanden hat,
darf Mitglied der «Kroko-
dile» werden. Wie kann sich
der querschnittgelähmte Kurt
bewähren?

Lukas Hartmann
So eine lange Nase *Ferien
voller Zauberei*
(20804 / ab 9 Jahre)

Christine Nöstlinger
Die verliebten Riesen
(20471 / ab 10 Jahre)
Der Riese Satlasch ist auf der
Fahrt zu seiner Riesenbraut
Amanda, als ihm plötzlich
das Benzin ausgeht ...

MARIE-THÉRÈSE SCHINS

2 X PAPA

ODER: ZWISCHENFALL AUF DEM PAUSENHOF

Dagmar Scherf
Das Geisterradio
(20857 / ab 9 Jahre)
**Das Geheimnis der schwarzen
Puppe** *oder: Sara kommt
von weit her*
(20788 / ab 10 Jahre)

Marie-Thérèse Schins
**2 x Papa oder: Zwischenfall auf
dem Pausenhof**
(20773) ab 9 Jahre)
Was soll Rob machen, als
sein Klassenkamerad Klaus
auf dem Pausenhof vor all
den anderen sagt, Robs
Vater sei schwul? Stimmt,
sein Vater ist schwul. Aber
was das ist, wissen eigentlich
die wengisten Kinder so ganz
genau. Für Rob heißt es
unter anderem, daß er sich
den Papa mit dessen neuem
Freund teilen muß ...

Ein Gesamtverzeichnis aller
lieferbaren Titel der Reihe
rororo rotfuchs findet Ihr in
der *Rowohlt Revue* und im
rotfuchs Schnüffelbuch.
Beides gibt es kostenlos in
Eurer Buchhandlung.
Rowohlt im Internet:
www.rowohlt.de